Kill Me, Kiss Me

A Novella

Kristina Stangl

ISBN: 978-1-963232-13-4

First Edition

Cover Art: FracinneaShelves

Library of Congress Registration Number: TXU002503324

Printed in the United States of America

Also by Kristina Stangl

The Enchanted Forest Saga:

The Curse of the Dark Horseman

The Sleeping Knight

The Emerald Prince

Silverheart:

Cupid's Serenade

Sex, Lies & Politics:

The Ambassador's Wife

Wake Up, Darling

My Life is a Soap Opera

Kill Me, Kiss Me

www.kristinastangl.com

DEDICATION

In dedication to my loving family. Thank you for your endless support.

To my readers, thank you for reading my books.

CONTENTS

Synopsis

Kill me or kiss me, sometimes, the only way to gain a husband's attention is to kidnap him…

Twelve years ago, they got married. As childhood friends, Kayla Steuber and Jack Warner came from opposite worlds. While she was born with a wooden spoon and raised by her grandmother out in a remote cabin in the woods; he was born with a silver spoon and grew up within his family's esteemed estate, Cerulean Manor.

However, in a twist of fate, Kayla is struck by an unexpected illness and is forced to marry her childhood friend. *A marriage rooted in paper.* But as Jack departs for the east coast to attend college, Kayla is left behind at Cerulean Manor to endure the cruel abuse spawned by her mother-in-law, Vivian Warner, and her household staff. Desperate to flee from her unfortunate fate, Kayla reluctantly accepts Vivian's offer to abandon her marriage and start a new life in another city.

Several years later, Kayla, an entrepreneur with a flower shop in San Francisco, is determined to move on from her estranged husband. After requesting for a divorce through an exchange of emails, Jack has chosen to ignore her. And now, as the newly elected Senator of California, it's become even more difficult to reach him. Furthermore, according to the press, Jack has a "wife" who lives overseas. Apart from her name, *Mrs. Warner*, not much else is known about the mysterious first lady.

Meanwhile, Jack's office has agreed to a billion-dollar project to renovate Kayla's community. Translation: In a matter of weeks, her local business will be forced to shut down and vacate the premise. Plus, after several unsuccessful attempts to reach him, Kayla is determined to confront Jack, once and for all. And to do so, she's willing to kidnap him. Force him to withdraw from the project and to at long last, divorce her for good.

But to Kayla's great surprise, when she finally comes face-to-face with her estranged husband, Jack simply laughs. Unfortunately, her gun failed to scare him off and furthermore, he claims that he still has no plans to divorce her. Apparently, the project only served as the aims to bring her back to him.

"Either, you kill me, now," he mischievously spoke, with a wicked grin resting upon his handsome face. "Or kiss me. Take your pick."

CHAPTER 1

Beautiful Things Are Deadly

"Kayla, isn't that your husband on television?" my assistant, Rebecca Fulton, curiously asks me as she intensely gazes at the screen. "Jack Warner has just won a seat at the senate. Doesn't this make you a senator's wife, now?"

"*Estranged husband,*" I promptly emphasize. "Besides, his business is *not* my business."

Twelve years ago, I married Jack Warner. Back then, we were eighteen years old and fresh out of high school. While I was a poor orphan born with a wooden spoon and raised by my widowed grandmother, Dorothy Steuber; Jack, on the other hand, was born with a silver spoon and grew up surrounded by wealth beyond measure. Had we lived in Europe during the Regency or Victorian eras, then he would have been a part of nobility. Most likely, *a duke*. But instead, in modern times, he was the heir to the Warner fortune, one of the wealthiest families originating from Portland, Oregon.

In fact, his family owned several mines scattered across the state of Oregon. Many of which, housed various precious gemstones, such as obsidian, jasper, agate, as well as gold and silver. Furthermore, while his father, Sylas Warner, was often away on business, Jack remained at home at his family's estate known as Cerulean Manor.

Our fates should never have intertwined. But, as destiny would have it, we met one summer out in the forest during our youth.

One day, while visiting the river by my home, I spotted a young boy standing in front of an archway, which was covered with a garland of wild belladonnas. His hair was platinum blonde like corn, along with rosy cheeks, a fair porcelain skin, and eyes as green as the evergreen forest which surrounded my cabin.

Dressed in a pair of olive-green cargo shorts, with a matching silk vest and a white buttoned-down cotton blouse, along with dark brown leather loafers, Jack Warner was the most beautiful creature that my young eyes had ever beheld before.

Even then, as a child, I knew that I was no match for the young lord. With my messy honey-brown hair, cobalt blue eyes, fair skin and clothes that were clearly out of fashion, overly worn and not to mention, handsewn by my grandmother; I wasn't the type of girl who was meant to mingle with the likes of him.

But, as he silently stood underneath those lovely and enchanting belladonnas— which ironically, was also my favorite flower growing up— even at the age of ten, I already foresaw that he was destined to be the death of me. This pretty thing that I so secretly loved and admired from afar, was fated to ruin me.

However, the moment our eyes first locked, to my surprise, I saw his alpine green eyes light up, instantly. Without second guessing, that beautiful boy ran over to my side and before I knew it, we became childhood friends. *Best friends.* An inseparable pair, who spent the entire summer frolicking through the grassy fields, climbing up trees, picnicking by the river, fishing, reading, cloud counting and even, rowing canoes together. In the end, we were like two peas in a pod.

Years later, as we entered into our teenage years, I presumed that we'd have gone on our own separate ways. Like flowers who blossom in the spring, only to wither away during the fall. However, unlike flowers, Jack was the exception to this rule; because, he never actually left my side. Rather, he simply refused to abandon me.

As lovely as he was, Jack could have had any other girl in town. With the passing of the seasons, that pretty boy grew up to become a strikingly handsome young man. Overnight, Jack grew tall and standing just shy over six feet and five inches. Meanwhile, his youthful face matured, with his jawline becoming sharper and more defined. Additionally, his brows thickened; his lips became more plump and pink; and his perfect Grecian nose became even more noticeable.

Furthermore, his boyish body transformed as well. Within the blink of an eye, Jack became more muscular and fit. Moreover, thanks to our time spent under the sun, his hair remained as blonde as ever. And lastly, his signature alpine green eyes, were still as dreamy as the first time I laid eyes upon him, all those many years ago.

Meanwhile, I, the tomboy girl from the woods, grew into a young and independent woman. Unlike Jack, not much had changed about my overall appearance. I still wore the same outdated, overly worn and handsewn dresses made by my grandmother. My honey-brown hair was still a long and tangled mess. If anything, Jack had blossomed into an enchanting beauty, while I stayed much of the same. A velvet rose next to a thorny shrub. And rather than trading me in for another girl; he instead, foolishly kept me all to himself.

But sadly, one day, I got sick. After a difficult winter, I caught a severe case of pneumonia. In fact, I was so ill that I almost died in my hospital bed. Furthermore, due to our struggling financial circumstances, with my aging grandmother on a fixed income received from government assistance, we had no available funds for my treatment.

However, miraculously, in a twist of fate, Jack suddenly appeared at my bedside as my savior. Using his family's powerful name and influence, he took it upon himself to save me.

By forcing the local priest to marry us in my sick bed, with my grandmother serving as a witness, Jack finally claimed me as his. To cover my medical costs and add me to his health insurance, he married me. And so, this is ultimately, how Jack Warner became my husband.

A few months later, I eventually healed from my illness. Afterwards, I was moved into Cerulean Manor, leaving my grandmother behind in our faithful cabin. But by then, Jack had already departed to attend college on the east coast. Thereupon, leaving me behind and in the care of his mother, Vivian Warner, in their family's ancestral estate.

If this was a fairy tale story, then this should have been my happily ever after. Cinderella finally marrying the wealthy and dashing prince. Except, sadly, in real-life, my life wasn't a fairy tale. In fact, it was the complete *opposite*.

It was the opposite outcome, because Vivian Warner *hated me*. The short, chin-length and platinum blonde hair matriarch with a thick and straight line of bangs, who wore a full face of makeup— including a thick layer of black mascara over her russet brown eyes and dressed in only exclusive designer clothes with bright red painted lips and matching nails, along with her signature Christian Louboutin heels— detested the girl who wore handsewn and raggedy clothes. A lonesome country girl, whom she believed was nothing more than the orphan *gutter rat* from the slums, who had somehow managed to seduce her darling son. According to her, I was...

Kayla Steuber, a gold-digging social climber.

Not only did Vivian despise me, but so did all her servants, too. Each day, they either ignored my entire existence, or they chose to recognize me only to belittle me. From mocking me by calling me cruel names, or serving me days old and stale food, to refusing to change my dirty bedsheets or returning my clothes from the laundry back in tatters— each moment of every passing day, they all made my life a living hell.

And if I didn't die on the hospital bed back when I was ill, then my new mother-in-law made it her personal business to make me wish that I had. Cursing me daily, for having dared to marry her beloved son. A man who should have remained beyond my reaches.

Apart from the ongoing harassment and vulgar jokes spoken directly to my face, Vivian and her maids forced me to drink an herbal cup of tea, served each day precisely at noon. And if it hadn't been for the mere fact that belladonnas were my all-time favorite flower that I had frequently admired out in the woods, then I never would have been able to recognize its unique smell, stemming from my tea.

Tragically, my mother-in-law was determined to see the end of me. Even if it meant poisoning me daily to force my early death and thereby, abandoning her son.

Luckily, while the maids were not looking, I was able to secretly dump the tampered tea into the grounds of a snake plant kept inside the far corner of my bedroom. But eventually, the fact that I was *still alive*, soon caught Vivian's attention a few weeks later.

Between my survival and Jack's absence from the manor, Vivian decided to take it upon herself to get rid of me, once and for all. After living at the estate for two whole months, she finally cornered me one evening after dinner. With much force, she proceeded to slap me hard, relentlessly. Within seconds, she violently beat me, until my face and body were severely swollen and bruised.

Afterwards, she offered me a deal. Stay and perish miserably under her watch, or take a million dollars and leave quietly.

As much as I cared for my childhood friend, I knew that I, a poor and lonely orphan, was no match to be the rightful wife that Jack Warner deserved. From his birth, Jack was groomed to be the heir to his family's fortune. A future CEO or a politician in the making. Someone like him deserved to have a better wife. A wife, who also came from his same upscale origins, with a far better pedigree than I.

Someone, who wasn't me.

Sadly, with a heavy heart, I took Vivian's offer and ultimately, chose *my freedom*. Either way, if I stayed behind, then I was destined to die. If not from the poisoned tea, then by some other violent means. In the end, Vivian Warner *always* got what she wanted.

And what she wanted above all else, was to see me gone.

Afterwards, I left Portland for good and moved further south to San Francisco. And on that fateful night, I packed a small suitcase, bid farewell to my grandmother and then, took an overnight Greyhound bus to start my new life. Shortly thereafter, I rented out an apartment and a year later, I opened a flower shop in the floral district of downtown San Francisco.

Eventually, Jack discovered my departure. Desperately, he wrote me countless emails, begging me to return back to Cerulean Manor. However, I didn't have the heart to reveal to him about what his mother and staff did to me. Nor, of Vivian's offer. Sadly, I didn't have the courage to face my childhood friend with the heart-wrenching truth.

Instead, I replied to ask for a divorce. And with that one single word, *divorce*, all communications ceased between him and I. Needless to say, I never heard from Jack, ever again. Not even a single email to date.

Now, twelve years later, I'm still *legally his wife*; although, I have no idea how he's doing. Has he moved on? Had other girlfriends? Children?

Perhaps, or perhaps not. Secretly, over the years, I've followed his political career in the press. After graduating from Harvard, he went on to run his father's company for a few years, before transitioning into politics. And as of tonight, he's just won the senate seat for California.

"According to the press, they say that Senator Warner has a wife," my perky redhead assistant stares at me, as she places a bouquet of red roses into a glass vase.

"But," she adds, "His wife is a bit of a mystery. They say that she lives overseas. She's only known in the press as *Mrs. Warner.*"

"Ha," I laugh to myself. "You know, Rebecca, I've never once been referred to as Mrs. Warner. Even his own family, never acknowledged me as such."

"It's their loss," Rebecca scowls. "They should have treated you right, from the very beginning. But Kayla, now that Jack is the newly elected Senator of California, what are you going to do?"

"Nothing," I quickly reply. "Jack and I are now strangers to each other. We might still be married on paper, but I doubt that he'd want anything to do with me at this point."

"But if that's the case, then why didn't you get a divorce? What's the point of still being married?"

"I don't know," I sigh aloud, as I arrange a bouquet of belladonnas with my gloved hands.

Staring at the belladonnas, which ironically, is the same name of my flower shop, I tell Rebecca, "Sometimes, beautiful things are deadly."

CHAPTER 2

Wedding Bell Blues

After Jack was sworn into office a few months ago, my own business bloomed, too. Not only was I busy overseeing the floral arrangements for a long list of weddings, but I also managed to score one of the biggest clients of the year: the wedding of rising star Katherine Sharp and her groom-to-be and billionaire tech guru, James Petruchio.

Ironically, Katherine is the former female candidate who previously lost the last election to my husband. According to the press, the election results were a devastating blow to her political career, in which she lost by a huge landslide. Not only did my estranged yet handsome husband manage to charm the voters at the ballot box, but he also succeeded on claiming victory with high flying colors, too.

Personally, I actually felt sorry for Katherine. After all, I, of all people, knows better than anyone else on earth, as to just how difficult it is to go against the likes of Jack Warner. For starters, Jack was and still is, perfect in every possible way. From looks to wealth, to intellect to charm, Jack Warner has always been destined for success. No one can ever compete with him. Especially, in an election.

Therefore, it came as no surprise to me, when I read in the papers about how badly Katherine lost to Jack. And deep down inside, I also sympathized with her, too.

To have your dreams stolen from right underneath your feet is never an easy truth to swallow. Having experienced my own struggles in the past, I understood firsthand with the challenges of letting go and the importance of starting over again.

That's why when my assistant, Rebecca, informed me about Katherine's interest on employing our services for her upcoming wedding, I jumped at her offer. Even though I recognize that I'm probably the last person on earth who's qualified to serve as the head florist to a woman who was once the political opponent to my husband; however, in the end, I decided to keep my true identity as a secret.

After all, I haven't seen Jack in well over twelve years. Therefore, why reveal my estranged husband's identity to Katherine and her team? Besides, I'm practically a divorced woman as it is!

And so, this is why and how Rebecca and I ended up as invited guests at Katherine's and James' wedding.

As the head florist of this event, I was in charge of decorating the wedding venue with the best flowers in town. Given that this wedding is held at Golden Gate Park, I opted to decorate the venue with hundreds of yellow roses in bloom— a personal favorite of the bride.

Meanwhile, the guest tables are decorated with crystal glass vases, consisting of fresh bouquets of white lilies of the valley and baby pink carnations. Furthermore, there are dozens of garlands consisting of crimson red and soft white roses spread across the park, covering most of the archways.

"The groom seems to be bestowed with his new bride," Rebecca sighs.

Being the hopeless romantic that she is, Rebecca always admires happy couples in love from afar. Truly, it's amazing that she's still single. Considering how much of an advocate she is of true love; by now, you'd think that Rebecca would have found her own Prince Charming.

"They do seem to love each other," I agree, as I take a sip of my white wine. "Her new husband certainly spent a fortune on this wedding. Especially, given the ridiculously expensive check that he wrote to us to cover the costs for these flowers."

"Well, he is a tech billionaire, after all," Rebecca reminds me.

"Wasn't he her assistant before?" I ask, curiously. "Or, something along those lines? At least, that's what I recall from the papers."

"Yes, it's true. He was her assistant," she clarifies. "But he only worked as her assistant, in order to be near her."

"So, was he already a secret billionaire?" I narrow my eyes in anticipation.

If true, then even I must admit, James' actions are rather romantic.

"Yes! He was!" Rebecca gushes. "By night, he secretly worked at his billion-dollar company, and by day, he served as her assistant. Apparently, James masqueraded as Katherine's assistant, so that he could woo her. In the end, it worked. And so, here we are, now attending their wedding as guests."

"So, they fell in love after the election," I deduce. "I guess sometimes in life, we can still find happiness. Even, in the midst of an existential crisis."

"Yes, it's true," Rebecca confirms. "According to James, it was a difficult time of adjustment for Katherine. Not only did she lose the election, but she also broke up with former fiancé, Luca Cambio. But eventually, over time, she got over it and found her true path. Now, she's happily married and owns an art gallery."

"I admire her for having the strength and courage to overcome her obstacles," I admit aloud. "To find love again after such loss, it's truly remarkable. A real inspiration for us all."

Gazing straight at my eye, Rebecca asks me, "Well, what about you?"

"What about me?" I shrug.

"Have you ever thought about remarrying? Finding love again?" she asks. "After all, you're still young. You're only thirty."

Although I'm taken aback by her question; however, I also know that Rebecca only wants what's best for me. From the outside view, it is strange that a thirty-year-old woman hasn't moved on from her ex. Especially, given the fact that our estrangement has lasted well over twelve years and counting.

However, the truth is that I've never been with anyone else other than Jack. Maybe, that's why I just can't imagine being with anyone else. Even if this decision makes me fated to be alone for the rest of my life, then so be it.

"My business is plenty enough to keep me busy for years to come," I tell her. "Besides, technically, I'm already married."

It might not be the best answer; however, it's still, nonetheless, the truth.

"But that hardly counts!" Rebecca scowls. "It's a paper marriage. No, you need… *deserve* to be with someone else, right *now*. A man who can fill your life with endless joy and comfort."

"I already have joy and comfort in my life," I correct her. "And, more importantly, I don't need a man to have fulfillment. Belladonna is enough for me."

While it's true, technically, as a strong and independent woman, I don't need a man to complete my life. I can stand on my own two feet, all on my own, thank you very much. Besides, it's pointless to reflect about my lost love with Jack. He might have been my first love, but we simply weren't destined to be.

"Enough about me," I attempt to change the subject. "What about you? Aren't you dating someone?"

"Ah… how did you know?" Rebecca blushes, turning bright red out of embarrassment.

Although she's courageous when inquiring about my love life; however, when the tables are turned around in reverse, she's too shy about herself. However, in my opinion, she shouldn't be.

In reality, Rebecca is a beautiful young woman in her early twenties, with a slender figure, deep marine blue eyes and flaming red hair. And as lovely and well-manner as she is, both inside and out, Rebecca is also a good-hearted country girl from the south, who fails to recognize just how pretty she is. A real southern belle.

"These past few weeks, you've been leaving the shop extra early before closing time," I casually point out. "Of course, it's not a problem. After all, your personal life is yours alone. However, naturally, I just assumed that maybe you were secretly dating someone after hours."

"Okay, you got me," she sighs in defeat. "I was trying to keep it a secret for a while, just because I wasn't sure if we were that serious."

"And?" I ask, with a raise brow.

"Well… we're serious now," she reveals, with a bright smile. "Simon asked me to move in with him last week. And I agreed."

"That's wonderful!" I happily exclaim.

Truly, I can't be any more thrilled for my best friend.

"I think I might marry him one day," she confesses.

"Well, if you do," I begin, "Then, please make sure that you hire me as your florist. I promise to decorate your wedding like a magical garden. And of course, it'll be free of charge."

"No!" she quickly exclaims.

"No?" I ask in surprise.

Is it possible that I might have offended her somehow?

"You won't be decorating my wedding, because you're going to be a part of it!" she clarifies.

"Part of your wedding? As in, a bridesmaid?" I blink in surprise.

"Maid of honor," she proudly smiles.

Instantly, I'm touched by her words. Sadly, I haven't actually been a party to a wedding before. Heck, I never even had a real wedding of my own. I was never a true bride who walked down the aisle, while wearing a white dress.

Instead, my wedding was held at the local hospital, with my grandmother serving as the only witness, along with the priest and a nurse who happened to be in the room. And now, having been asked to be a part of her wedding ceremony, it truly is touching.

"It would be a sincere honor to serve as your maid of honor," I proudly smile, with a tear streaming down my eye.

"Don't start crying on me!" she yells. "He hasn't even asked me to marry him, yet!"

"Well, if he doesn't ask soon, then he's an idiot," I laugh on, as I wipe my tears away with a handkerchief.

"Thank you," Rebecca warmly smiles.

"By the way," she adds on, "Simon has an older brother, too. Care to meet him?"

"Unless, he's a gardener who can provide me with an endless supply of flowers, then I'm not interested," I tease.

"Very well, then the next time I see David, I'll tell him to start gardening."

After the wedding ceremony, I decide to stop by Belladonna to finish a few more floral arrangements for the upcoming week. Since my apartment is located in the same building as my flower shop, I'm often able to get ahead of my work due to the convenient commute.

However, as I approach my building, I notice a large crowd gathered and standing in the middle of the street. Recognizing a few faces from amongst the crowd, I realize that most of these folks are my neighbors.

"Mrs. Wong, what's going on?" I ask my elderly neighbor of twelve years.

Like me, Mrs. Wong is also an entrepreneur who lives and owns a restaurant in my building.

"Oh, Kayla!" she exclaims, with a worried expression. "Everyone is upset about these pink notices. The city posted it on all of our windows and doorways."

"What notice?" I ask her, now worried about this unexpected announcement.

"Don't you know?" she asks me in return; surprised, that I'm the only resident ignorant about this important news.

"No, I've just come back from a wedding," I explain.

"Oh dear, then you really, don't know," she shakes her head.

"Know what?" I press on.

"The government is planning to tear down our building!" Mrs. Wong shouts, with anger. "According to the pink flyers posted outside of our windows and doors, the city plans to convert our building and the surrounding neighborhood into a new shopping mall!"

Instantly, I abandon Mrs. Wong's side and flee to my shop. And sure enough, there resting above Belladonna's store front window is a notice. A bright pink flyer with black lettering written on it. It reads as follows:

To the Resident/Owner of this Establishment:

Please take notice that effective at the end of this month, your building will be permanently closed. After much deliberation and review, the city and state governments have decided to renovate this neighborhood in compliance with Project Bluebird, led by Senator Jack Warner. Our goal is to make San Francisco a more safe, healthy and smart city for the people of tomorrow.

Compensation not exceeding $10,000 will be provided to all residents and business owners residing within this neighborhood.

Regards,

The City and County of San Francisco

After reading this notice, I've taken away five important key facts. One, I will lose my business. Two, I will also lose my home. Three, $10,000 is hardly enough funds to cover any moving expenses. Four, that my estranged husband is behind this project.

And five, being the most important key fact above all else: I can no longer afford to ignore my husband.

After twelve long years, the time has finally come to face him. Whether I wish to or not, come heaven or hell, I must confront Jack Warner, once and for all!

CHAPTER 3

The Solution is Kidnapping

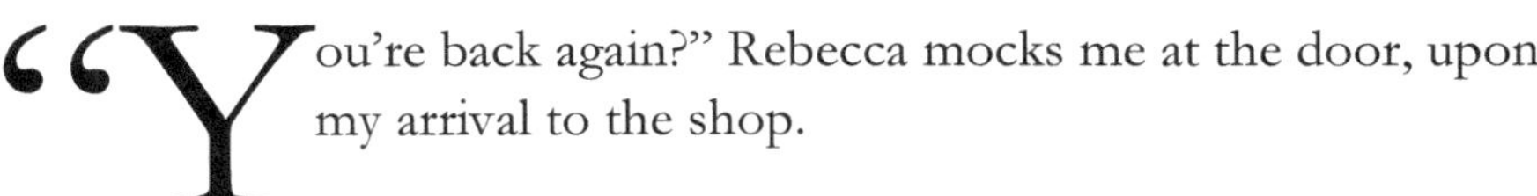

"You're back again?" Rebecca mocks me at the door, upon my arrival to the shop.

"What can I say? I simply cannot get an appointment to see him," I sigh out of frustration.

After spending my entire morning couped up inside the waiting room of Jack's office, I was practically ready to fall asleep in my chair out of sheer boredom. If it wasn't for the fact that his secretary, Shirley Ross, alerted me that Jack had stepped out of his office for lunch, then I still would have been waiting there in his office, right now.

"Well, did you ever consider telling his secretary that you're his wife? Surely, a wife should be given higher priority to visit her husband without a scheduled appointment?"

"I just can't seem to form those words within my mouth," I admit in earnest. "Telling people that I'm his wife, feels like it's a disgraceful lie."

"But it's not a lie!" she shouts. "You are *his wife!*"

"Rebecca, I haven't seen him in twelve years," I point out. "Besides, even if he saw my face, Jack might not even recognize me, anymore."

"No, Senator Warner will definitely recognize you," Rebecca reassures me. "You're too beautiful to be forgotten. It's probably why he never divorced you in the first place."

"Me, beautiful? Ha!" I huff, sarcastically.

"You are beautiful, Kayla," she tells me. "You're just too modest. That's your problem."

"Well, pretty or not, my looks aren't getting me an appointment to see him," I sigh, as I collapsed down onto the sofa.

"So, what do you plan to do?"

"I guess, I'll just have to return back to his office and try again tomorrow."

"Why not try calling him, or sending him an email or something?" she suggests.

"First of all," I begin, "Jack stopped responding to my emails, twelve years ago. And second, his phone line is busy. I already tried. I think the whole neighborhood must have been calling his phone line like crazy, ever since they got their pink notices."

"Plus," I add on, "It was a miracle that I was even allowed to enter into his waiting room, unannounced. His entire floor was already flooded with a sea of people."

"Shouldn't he be stationed at the capital in Sacramento?" Rebecca points out.

"According to Shirley, he also has an office in San Francisco," I inform her. "Apparently, he prefers his office, here in the city. Plus, I guess with this new renovation project, Jack has made it his business to be stationed primarily in downtown San Francisco. At least, for the time being."

"Gosh, this does sound frustrating," Rebecca sympathizes. "It's almost as if you need to kidnap him or something, in order to speak with him."

Suddenly, the lights go off in my head. *Kidnapping.* Maybe, just maybe, that's the answer. After twelve long years, Jack has deliberately ignored me. Every email. Phone call. Letter.

Nothing.

As a wife, I've long accepted his silence as a form of atonement for my past sins. Endless guilt, aimed at my betrayal for abandoning our marriage, without ever having the decency to tell him the real reason as to why I left him in the first place.

But now, if kidnapping is the only solution to my woes, then perhaps, this ignored wife is ready to commit the most impossible crime, after all.

At the stroke of noon, I arrive to the parking lot located right outside of Jack's building. According to Shirley, he leaves the office for lunch each day promptly at noon.

After paying off his driver a hefty sum, I was able to borrow a chauffeur's uniform and sneak into the car as Jack's driver for the day.

In this disguise, I'm hoping that I can finally have a heart-to-heart conversation with my estranged husband. God willing, our long-awaited reunion can solve all my woes, including the issues revolving my business, residence and most importantly, *our marriage.*

And if not, then I've got a shiny new revolver, which I previously bought from a local pawn shop that's currently hidden away inside of my pocket… just in case things don't exactly go according to my plans…

CHAPTER 4

Kill Me, Kiss Me

For twelve long and agonizing years, I desperately yearned for this moment. A chance to see her, once more. Whether it's a knife held to my chest or a hug, I'll take any reaction from her. Hate me or love me, it doesn't matter. As long as I can see her… touch her… even for a split second… then that's all that matters to me in the end…

Right now, I, Jack Warner, am seated behind in the backseat of my limousine, with my estranged wife posing as my driver. She might have been clever to arrange this unorthodox reunion; however, unfortunately for her, my men are also loyal to me.

As it turns out, Charles, my driver, was only too quick to inform me that my long-term plans have finally come into fruition. Kayla might have thought that she had the upper hand in this chase; but in reality, she only fell into the trap that I personally laid out for her. Like a bluebird finally stepping into its customed built bird cage.

The woman, whom I've spent most of my entire life adoring and loving from afar, has finally found her way back to me. From the first moment I laid eyes upon her as a young boy, I instantly knew that she was my soulmate.

And now, I can't help but smile. Even as her hostage, I'll gladly surrender my life to her in an instant. Die right here, in this very car, if it means that I can see her one last time. Sell my soul to the very devil himself, if it gives me the chance to settle our disputes, once and for all.

To kiss her for the very last time.

Because my life has never been the same, ever since she left. Without any notice or a valid reason, she abandoned our marriage and disappeared from my life, completely. Within the blink of an eye, she left me cold and dry, and even had the audacity to ask for a divorce. Not that I'd ever give her one. She'd have to murder me in cold blood, for that to ever happen.

Even with my last ounce of breath, I'd never divorce her. She'd sooner become a widow, before a divorcee. Because in the end, I waited a lifetime for her.

And most important, Kayla is mine.

At first sight, I vowed to myself that she'd be my bride. That day, when we first met outside in the forest, I was captivated by her. With her long honey-brown hair, cobalt blue eyes and fair skin, she was a beauty that was kept hidden away from the rest of the world.

Between her worn out clothes, unkept hair, fierce and wild spirit, Kayla was a like small bird, whom only *I* could care for. Uncorrupted by the evil world that surrounded us. An innocent, enchanting and lovely bluebird that belonged solely to *me.*

Growing up, no one really understood her, except for me. Kayla was never a popular one; but I preferred her that way. I liked that I was her only friend. That together, we were each other's world, out in the middle of the forest.

Just her and me.

When we were eighteen years old and Kayla got sick, I was about ready to die. If she didn't survive, then I was going to join her in the next world by any means necessary. Poison. Gunshot. Hanging.

Neither method mattered.

Luckily, for both our sakes, she survived. And by then, we were already wed and proclaimed as man and wife.

Originally, I had planned on attending Harvard for only a semester, before returning home to Oregon to bring Kayla back with me to the east coast. For us to move into a small apartment, while I attended school. However, by the time I returned back to Cerulean Manor during my winter break, she was already gone.

And my entire world as I knew it was shattered.

"She left you," is what Vivian told me. "Left you out cold. Best to forget about her and move on."

Except, such a notion was impossible. To forget Kayla? *My precious Kayla?*

To erase the burning and all-consuming love that I hold for her and only her? To move on from the only woman, whom I have ever loved my entire life, with all fiber of my being? I'd sooner hang myself, before allowing such a reality to take hold!

And so, I tracked her down. Secretly, I stalked Kayla in San Francisco. For six whole months, I followed her each day, as she traveled around town and worked at her flower shop, Belladonna. By then, I was also communicating with her via online through an exchange of emails. Desperately, trying to convince her to come back home to Oregon.

To return to me.

But then, she wrote those heart-wrenching words that I barely have the strength to repeat. *Divorce.* Had I not loved her so passionately and fiercely, then I'd sooner kill her. I would much rather slice both of our necks with a sharpened knife, before I'd ever give her up.

And so, I gave Kayla her space. Allowed her the chance to temporarily stretch her wings and have the freedom to fly and grow. And while I hoped that she'd come back to me freely out of her own free will, like a bird returning home to their owner after a season of traveling; tragically, Kayla failed to do so.

Instead, she took too long.

After that last email, I returned back to Harvard and finished the rest of my studies. Afterwards, I spent a few years working for my father, before taking over the mining business. However, Kayla still never returned to me.

In the years that passed, she never made the effort to write or call me back. Nor, visit her aging grandmother who still lived in town.

Luckily, I hired a private detective to watch over her and keep tabs on her whereabouts. Every Wednesday at noon, I'd receive a weekly report about her. Thank the heavens above, she remained faithful to me. Even during our separation, she never took in another lover. For if she had, then I would have easily been a murderer.

For over a decade, I lived my life, constantly watching over Kayla from the shadows. Every milestone, celebration, and joy that she experienced in her life, I watched them all from behind the scenes through pictures and videos.

But eventually, in time, I began to grow impatient. After ten years of separation, I decided that I needed to do *something* to finally gain her attention. To have my estranged bluebird fly back to me.

To its rightful owner.

And so, on Kayla's twenty-eight birthday, that was the day that

I decided to go into politics.

I knew that if I wasn't in the public eye, then Kayla would never pay attention to my whereabouts. And so, I used my family's connections and secured an internship at the Governor's Office in Sacramento, the capital city to the state where my beloved resides in.

For a year, I learned the political ropes by working directly under the governor, who was an old friend of my father. With his support, I was able to secure a senate nomination and ran against my opponent, Katherine Sharp, with flying colors.

After winning the election and securing my position as the new Senator of California, my plans were finally set in motion. Shortly, thereafter, I moved my offices out west to San Francisco and authored Project Bluebird.

Although the plan aimed on renovating an impoverish neighborhood in the city under the banner of promoting new social and technological developments for the community; the real truth is that I knew it'd also be the means to reunite me with Kayla.

Unfortunately, if being the villain is the only way for me to bring Kayla back into my orbit, then so be it. Threatening to close down her business and evict her from her home is something that I'll gladly do, if it means that she'll finally return back to me.

And at long last, my gamble paid off. Because right now, she's here, as my driver. Heaven finally decided to bless this bastard, after all.

Suddenly, the car takes a detour off the freeway and proceeds to travel down a dirt road. Wherever she is taking me, she's searching for an isolated location.

My adrenalin is in full motion, and my heart begins to flutter. Finally, finally, *finally*, she's going to confront me. Yell at me. Beat me. Do *anything* to me.

Whatever you do Kayla, please, just don't walk away from me…

And then, at long last, the car comes to a halt. We are now parked underneath a birch tree, located near Golden Gate Park. With no one else around us, Kayla lowers the driver's window, exposing her face towards my direction.

And at long last, our eyes finally meet.

Kayla is as beautiful as I last remembered her to be. In fact, she's even lovelier than I imagined. Her blue eyes are sparkling, her cheeks are rosy, her lips are soft and delicate and her pale skin, remains as flawless as ever. Even in her disguise, with a driver's cap covering her front honey-brown locks, I can still see traces of her signature hair from her sides and tucked behind her ear.

Oh, how I missed her.

But our reunion is not a happy one. At least, from her side. Right now, she has a shiny and silver revolver that's dangling within her hands. And to my misfortune, it's aimed right towards my chest.

"Forfeit Project Bluebird," she spouts as her first set of words, spoken to me in well over twelve years.

As much as I would have preferred to hear the words, *I love you,* from her; however, I'm not that delusional. It's going to take me some time to win her over, again. And as God as my witness, I will win her heart, once more.

"And while we're at it," Kayla glares at me, as she shoves her gun deeper towards my chest. "Divorce me, too."

Ah, that *word,* again. *Divorce.* After all these years apart, it seems that my wife still hasn't accepted her fate as of yet. But don't worry, my precious Kayla. I will set things right again. Nevertheless, I'm still tickled by this long-awaited reunion.

"Well, love, with that gun of yours, either, you kill me, now," I happily smile from ear-to-ear, as I grab a hold of her hand and shove the gun even deeper towards my chest. "Or kiss me. Take your pick."

Judging by her expression, she's surprised by my reaction. However, that surprise does not last long. Soon enough, it's replaced with anger.

"You really are a bastard!" Kayla shouts out of frustration, as she decides to lower her gun an inch down. "Even in the face of danger, you still refuse to take me seriously!"

"Better to pull the trigger than to wave it carelessly, don't you think?" I tease her, happily.

Already, her hands are shaking. From the looks of it, she's not accustomed to holding a gun. Ah, my little bluebird. Your chirp is worse than your bite.

"But, I'll tell you what," I attempt to comfort her. "I'm willing to make a proposition with you."

"A proposition? With me?" her beautiful blue eyes sparkle with hope.

Eyes that I've desperately longed to stare into for years on end.

"I'm a powerful man," I remind her. "One word from me, and I can make all of your dreams come true."

And then to my upmost pleasure, I wink at her.

"Just like that, you're willing to help me?" she blinks in disbelief.

Her reaction is funny. Does she truly not realize that I would do anything for her? Absolutely, *anything?*

But, right now, I will not humor her. No, she needs to acknowledge her identity, first. She must remember who she is. Who I am. Who *we* are. No more running away. After all, she is *my wife.*

"And who are you?" I casually pose my question over to her.

Although it's obvious who she is, I still must taunt my little bluebird. After all, I've missed her sweet melodies for years on end.

And if my bluebird wants to come in disguised as my driver, well, then, I'll gladly humor her, too.

"After all, I don't make deals with strangers," I inform her, with a wicked smile. "Especially, someone without a name."

For a second, she nervously stares at me. It's almost as if she's contemplating as to whether or not, I even recognize her after all these years.

Oh, my silly girl. Of course, I remember you. I've only thought about you for every second of each day for well over a decade.

"Kayla Steuber," she hesitates to say.

By now, her revolver is away from my direction and resting on the passenger's seat.

"Who?" I pressure her. *Steuber* is the wrong answer.

"Your childhood friend," she tries again.

"Come again?" I taunt her. Either way, her answer is still not good enough.

With a heavy sigh, she finally says the magical words: "Your wife."

"Ah, now I remember," I blissfully smile, approvingly. "Finally, you came."

Jack really is a bastard. He's as sneaky as ever. Not only does he have the upper hand in this deal of his, but I honestly don't have any other choice but to accept his proposal. After all, I've just foolishly and recklessly committed a crime by kidnapping him and threatening a gun over his head.

God, I'm so dumb!

But, thankfully, according to Jack, he's willing to drop the project altogether, as well as ignoring my attempted kidnapping scheme, so long as I return back to him as his wife.

No exceptions.

Translation: I will get to keep my flower shop and apartment, plus, all my neighbors will be okay too— so long as I return back to his side. But at this point, what does being by Jack's side mean anymore?

We've never actually lived together before, as a traditional husband and wife. Yes, we were childhood friends and have been legally married for the past twelve years; but all facts aside, does he want to have a real marriage with me? Sleeping in the same bed? Being in a real-life relationship as a true couple?

I hesitate to accept his proposition. But in reality, what other choice do I have? Perhaps, if I parade around as a horrible wife, then he'll later change his mind about us and agree to a divorce. However, knowing Jack, I highly doubt it.

Either way, I've got nothing to lose. And so, placing my revolver back into my pocket, I extend my hand over to my husband and accept his terms.

God help me.

CHAPTER 5

Mrs. Warner Revealed

Soon after my unorthodox reunion with Jack, I moved into his fancy downtown penthouse and thus, left my simple, peaceful and quiet life as a single flower shop owner behind me.

As part of our agreement, I'm to live with Jack as his wife. Which, in return, means that I'm no longer permitted to reside in my old apartment alone, nor to work at my flower shop full-time. At least, for the time being.

Luckily, Rebecca agreed to manage Belladonna's operations, while Mrs. Wong offered to watch over my apartment. Surprisingly, even as a florist, I never left any living plants inside of my home. Everything of value, I've kept it for safekeeping in my shop. Subconsciously, I suppose that deep down inside, I never felt like my San Franciscan apartment was ever going to be a permanent location for me.

One way or another, I guess I secretly knew that at some point, I was going to cross paths with my estranged husband again. Whether it was now or five years later, our meeting was inevitable.

However, never in a million years did I ever envision us living together. Instead, I always pictured a future with me divorced and living elsewhere, far away from his reaches. But in a twist of fate, here I am, reunited with my husband.

The day I aimed a gun to his heart, my fate was sealed. From that moment onwards, Jack took sole ownership of me— like a bird having been caught by its hunter.

After I accepted his proposal, Jack promptly escorted me back to my apartment. From there, he watched me like a hawk, as I packed a small suitcase with a few of my belongings. Afterwards, we departure for his penthouse. Being the control freak that he is, he even drove the limousine himself, fearful that I might forfeit our deal and try to flee again.

Except this time around, it really was too late. Even this foolish bluebird knew her own limits. One way or another, he finally caught me.

Eventually, once we arrived at Jack's home, his residence was exactly as I envisioned it would be. Just like Cerulean Manor, his penthouse resembled a palace. Indeed, not much had changed since the days of our childhood. His Californian abode might not have been his family's ancestral estate; however, it came as a close second.

Located on the top thirty-first floor, Jack's penthouse is three times larger than both my shop and apartment combined. At first glance, I notice that the setup is minimal in its design. There are no prestigious or expensive artworks out on display. Instead, Jack's apartment consists of a collection of basic furniture pieces, along with standard white walls and cream marbled floors.

Additionally, the penthouse also houses three private bedrooms, with direct access to their own personal balconies, which provides a spectacular view of the city; along with a medium sized kitchen, and a large and spacious living and dining room. Not to mention, there's also a butler, a housekeeper and a cook, who all resides on the first floor of our building.

Overall, Jack's home is the perfect palace-like residence for a billionaire bachelor, who clearly has no wife or children. Perhaps, during our decade spent apart, Jack really didn't keep a mistress, after all.

Much to my own relief, he didn't force me to share his bed. Instead, Jack gave me my own private room, with a brand-new wardrobe to go along with it. Clothing pieces that were designed and crafted by some of the world's top fashion designers. Chanel. Gucci. Versace. Herrera. Vuitton. Clothes that I previously only dreamt of wearing, are now, miraculously, all hanging within my new closet. And to top it all off, every outfit was tailored to match my exact size, too!

Just how on earth did Jack know my clothing size, even after all these years? Not to mention, I've also gained a few extra pounds since my teenage years!

Finally, after all these years, the Warner's life of luxury is staring before me, right in front of my face. *Wealth beyond measure.* A stark contrast to my old life as a single and struggling florist, living in one of the less-than-privileged sides of the city.

But as I gaze into the golden mirror of my new vanity, I still see the same face in the reflection. *My face.* The same long, honey-brown and untamed hair. The same bright cobalt blue eyes. The same pale complexion. *Me,* unfiltered.

The world around me might have drastically changed; however, I still remain unchanged. A rare oddity that clearly doesn't belong in Jack's upscale world. And yet, just like when we were children, he still wants me, either way.

And now, with me living underneath the same roof as Jack, God only knows what sort of future lies ahead of us.

For the past month, I've remained in Jack's penthouse... no correction... *our penthouse*, as he constantly clarifies this key fact to me on a daily basis. With Rebecca busy managing Belladonna's daily operations, I've been able to focus on transitioning into my new role as a senator's wife.

Apparently, mastering the role of Mrs. Warner is a lot more challenging than I initially anticipated. Since the moment I stepped into Jack's world, I've been ambushed by an entire entourage. And each of them, have all been striving to rewrite my life, as they rigorously train me on transitioning into my new role.

Starting with etiquette classes, I've been paired with the likes of Evelyn Decker, the top-tier professional etiquette trainer, who's known throughout high society as the woman who can transform even dirt-bound worms into floating and elegant butterflies.

Under Evelyn's wings, I've been trained on all sorts of things, which I previously never bothered to learn before. Values and traditions that I foolishly once thought weren't important to master. Apparently, as a country girl, I severely lacked the social grace, elegance and proper manners required for a political spouse to possess.

From my eating habits to my walking and posture; to my speech and conversational skills; I've been retrained on everything, like a child attending grade school and learning their alphabets for the very first time. According to Evelyn's feedback, everything I did seemed to be incorrect. From the way I held my spoon at the table, to how I previously used my cutlery to dissect my steaks with the dinner knife, to how I held my teacup with my pinky finger faced down— apparently, I was a total savage!

And so, every day for the past month, I've been forced to meet with Evelyn to relearn the refined manners that my grandmother apparently neglected to teach me back in the woods. But if my eating habits weren't bad enough, then my posture and overall grace, were greatly in need of elevation, too.

Therefore, Evelyn arranged for my daily equestrian, chess and dance lessons. According to her, these activities are designed to not only improve my physical posture, but to also sharpen my mind as well. Additionally, these recreational hobbies will also further enhance my conversational skills with the upper class. Apparently, high society just loves to talk about horses, chess and dancing— a stark contrast to the gossips and floral arrangement conversations that I used to share with Rebecca, Mrs. Wong and my grandmother.

As a result, Mondays are dedicated to my horseback riding lessons with my tutor, Ned Kingsley. Meanwhile, Wednesdays are allocated to chess lessons with chess champion, Brandon Hicks; and Thursdays are my dance lessons with world renowned ballroom dancer, Joyce Suthers.

Day by day, I've been slowly mastering each one of my tasks. For a shy tomboy who once had two left feet; somehow, during my rigorous training, I managed to dance the waltz and tango in one go!

Not to also mention, my equestrian skills have also vastly improved as well. From struggling to hop on a horse to riding a full mile around the track while on horseback, I've certainly come a long way. Plus, I also managed to beat Brandon on a few rounds of chess, too! Checkmate!

Lastly, there's my social etiquettes. At the stroke of three o'clock in the afternoon, I meet with Evelyn regularly for a daily session of high tea at the Ritz Carlton. Together, we practice on my conversational skills.

From how to properly smile and introduce myself to others, to how to politely inquire about one's private life, to how to gently decline an offer, and even, how to correctly stir my tea— apparently, I used to stir my tea in the wrong direction with my silver spoon! As Evelyn so eloquently informed me, "Kayla, it's left to right, not counterclockwise. And so on and so forth…"

Now, after much effort, I'm practically a new woman, fully transformed. Or, at least, that's how I feel in the inside.

Even though Jack gifted me with a brand-new wardrobe filled with high-end designer labels, I'm still hesitant to wear them. I might be the real Mrs. Warner, but deep down inside, I still feel like Kayla Steuber from Portland, Oregon. The tomboy, who grew up wearing raggedy and handsewn dresses, while frolicking barefoot out in the forest; before eventually, settling for secondhand clothes bought from city thrift stores.

Overall, I've lived most of life parading around as a hippie. A free spirt who cared less about her own physical appearance and more about flowers. Ask me the name of a flower, and I'll know the answer by heart. Even with a blindfold on, I can easily identify a white daisy, a bluebell, a sunflower or a marigold in an instant, all by its scent. However, quiz me on the latest gowns walking the runway and instantly, I'm at a loss for words.

Therefore, transitioning into a classically refined lady, who wears high fashion with the snap of a finger, is a huge leap for me. However, as a part of our agreement and as my role as Jack's wife, this little green bulb is finally blossoming into a red rose. I might be a late bloomer, but at least, I'm blooming.

And so, after three weeks of intense training, Evelyn arranged for me to meet with the famous stylist, Greta Winters. With the snip of her scissors, my long and tangled honey-brown hair is finally trimmed down, with an extra set of layers added to my ends. Now, my long honey-brown hair that once touched my knees, is shortened to reach the length of my elbows. Although my hair is technically still long;

however, this physical transformation is nevertheless, a huge transition for me.

Afterwards, Greta redoes my makeup, styles my hair and forces me to wear the clothes that Jack had previously gifted to me. And thus, with a simple change of hair, makeup and clothes, I'm fully transformed, like a butterfly.

Now, as I stare across into the mirror and admire my reflection on the other side, I'm finally ready to acknowledge that I'm no longer Kayla Steuber, anymore. One way or another, in a matter of a few weeks, I've somehow managed to fully transition into Kayla Warner.

Mrs. Warner.

And the thought of being Jack's wife… well… it doesn't feel all that bad, anymore.

Currently, it's eight o'clock in the evening, and I'm seated at the back table located in the ballroom to attend a black and white tie charity ball. Although we arrived separately, I'm still here to fulfill my part as Jack's supportive wife.

We might be married on paper, but thankfully, Jack continues to respect my personal space by allowing me to remain alone each night, within the privacy of my bedroom. Thus far, he hasn't pressured me for sex. Apart from our nightly dinners, I hardly see him. As the

Senator of California, Jack's a busy man, who often spends his time traveling back and forth between San Francisco, Sacramento and Washington, D.C.

Given our past estrangement, our first time seen together in public should feel awkward. But surprisingly, it doesn't. In fact, I'm actually enjoying my time spent in his company.

Thankfully, our conversations are light-hearted. Strangely enough, we're talking about our days, just like a normal married couple. And in these rare and special moments, I can't help but wonder what might have been had we not separated.

Had Vivian Warner not interfered in our marriage.

In the end, Jack Warner is still my childhood friend. We might be in our thirties now; but as I watch him smile and converse with me, I'm reminded that deep down inside, he's still the same boy that I grew up with back in the forest.

Moreover, Jack could have easily turned me in to the police's custody, after I kidnapped him. But instead, he spared me for no other reason than to protect me. In retrospect, since crossing paths with him again, my life has gotten a lot easier.

No longer am I struggling with my business. In fact, Jack paid off all of my debts and even went so far as to purchase my entire building. Now, both Belladonna and my apartment are fully paid off. Even Rebecca got a pay raise, too. Not to mention, Mrs. Wong now lives rent free in our building. Plus, Jack also paid off her restaurant's rent in full, too.

It's times like these that I'm reminded as to just how generous Jack really is. Even as children, he used to look after me back in the woods. When the kids from school used to pick on me because of my raggedy clothes and poor background, Jack always protected me. Often, beating up the students who dared to mess with the likes of me. Jack might have been the wealthiest kid in town, but he was also the bravest and strongest, too.

Just why did Jack leave me behind, when he left to attend college? Maybe, if he brought me with him all those years ago, then I would have stayed with him. Avoided the cruel abuse and torture by his heartless mother and her staff.

The horrors of Cerulean Manor.

However, brushing these negative memories aside; I must remain focused. Tonight, marks my first public appearance as Kayla Warner. In fact, as of recently, I stopping using my birth name, Kayla Steuber.

No longer are my bank accounts, business license or official documents listed under my maiden surname of Steuber. Thanks to Jack's lawyer, Julian Archer, all of my legal documents now reflects my married and legal name, Kayla Warner.

In honor of tonight's event, I'm dressed in a sapphire blue sequin mermaid form-fitting gown, with my honey-brown hair swept aside and secured into a long ponytail. With Greta's assistance, my eyelids have been smudged with a smokey shade of dark blue eyeshadow, while my lips have been painted with a fair shade of pink lipstick. Moreover, I'm sporting a diamond studded pair of earrings and on my wedding finger, I'm wearing a sapphire and diamond oval-shaped ring. A ring that ironically, matches my eyes, and my gown for the evening.

For the first time since marrying Jack, I'm actually wearing a ring around my finger. I know it's most likely all for show; however, I can't help but feel a bit sentimental about wearing it publicly, too.

The first ring that I ever got from Jack was when we were kids. One day, while out in the woods, he made me a ring crafted out of a string of white daisies, which he later placed around my finger.

At the time, we were fifteen years old and on that day, he

vowed to replace it in the future with a sapphire ring to match my eyes. In truth, I never actually took him seriously. However, in the end, Jack kept his word.

"Excuse me," Jack addresses the crowd at the podium on stage, after leaving my side at the table.

Since tonight's event is meant to serve as a charity ball aimed to help collect funds from wealthy donors to sponsor a college scholarship designed for underprivileged kids; Jack's speech is the official kick-off for the fundraiser.

And as a form of goodwill, Jack's former political opponent, Katherine Petruchio (née Sharp), will be voluntarily auctioning off her artwork at this charity event. Furthermore, all proceeds received from this auction, will be directed towards funding the college scholarship, known formally as Freedom Bluebird.

"Thank you all for coming," Jack speaks to the crowd. "Before we begin tonight's auction, I'd like to make an announcement."

Suddenly, the lights dim low, and I'm left wondering as to why that is.

"For years, many from the press have insistently inquired about the whereabouts concerning my wife," he playfully grins towards the mass sea of people.

His expression indicates mischief. It's a wicked grin that only Jack is the master of. Suddenly, my heart begins to race.

"And while, Mrs. Warner, has been traveling quietly abroad during my political campaign," he informs them, as his expression soon evolves into a blissful smile, which stretches from ear-to-ear, while his alpine green eyes shine brightly against the backdrop of the ethereal chandelier lights.

"But now," he proudly gazes at my direction, "My wife, has finally come home."

Instantly, our eyes lock and it feels like we're the only two souls in this entire room. However, a second later, Jack quickly snaps his fingers and instantly, a bright beam of light is shined directly upon me.

"Please give me your hands on honoring my wife, Kayla Warner," he orders the crowd.

"Mrs. Kayla Warner. *My wife*," he possessively declares, with a proud smile. A joyful smile, that I've never once witnessed upon his face before. Not in all the many years that I've known him.

He truly does look happy.

Meanwhile, as the spotlight shines brightly down upon me and the crowd relentlessly cheers away, I stare directly at Jack and observe the mirth that's currently resting upon his sweet and handsome face. Suddenly, like a lightbulb gone off, I finally comprehend the importance of this moment.

There is no escaping him.

Given the fact, that Mrs. Warner has finally been publicly revealed to be *me*; now, as a direct result, I will forever be chained to his man's side. At long last, Jack Warner has caught his cherish little bluebird, who once flew away from his reaches.

And now, after all these years flying solo, I'm truly his.

CHAPTER 6

Jack the Gunslinger

"Your aim sucks," Jack clicks his tongue in disapproval, while he loads a bullet into his shiny and silver revolver.

"I've never actually shot anything before," I confess aloud, feeling ashamed on how poorly I'm performing with this task.

"Not even, in the forest," I add on. "I've never hunted anything. Not a single bird."

"That's because you are a bird, Kayla," he wickedly grins. "My little bluebird."

And with that statement, Jack steadily holds his gun and aims straight ahead. With full confidence, he pulls the trigger and releases the bullet, piercing right through the target.

A perfect shot. Bullseye on one try.

"Now," Jack orders me, as he stands behind and attempts to get me into position.

After kidnapping my husband a few weeks ago, I've been forced to suffer the consequences of my poor actions.

First, I was ordered to relocate into my once estranged husband's penthouse. Second, I underwent extensive training to become a proper high society political wife. Third, the press got a hold of my real identity, curtesy of my now, very un-estranged husband. And now, as a result, my face has been plastered just about everywhere!

All the news magazines, gossip columns, tabloids, social media posts and various media outlets, have revealed the true identity and whereabouts of Mrs. Kayla Warner; and thus, making me the talk of the town. And according to the romanticized tale about my past, the headlines claims that me, Jack's mysterious wife, is none other than his high school sweetheart. A real rags-to-riches tale, with many dubbing me as a modern Cinderella.

Kaylarella.

It's funny how fast one's life can drastically change. From a lonely florist to a political spouse, my simple life has undergone an entire 360 degrees makeover, come overnight.

By now, I foolishly thought that Jack would have grown bored with me and thus, divorce me. But instead, it's the complete opposite. In fact, these days, I seem to be even more personally involved with his shenanigans, like tonight's activity.

Moreover, due to my poor kidnapping skills that I foolishly attempted to execute the last time; Jack is more determined than ever to have me properly trained with a revolver. According to him, our lives lived in the spotlight can at times, be dangerous.

Since everyone in the press knows our faces, as public figures, Jack wants me trained on how to properly use a gun. And surprise, surprise, surprise… he's volunteered to be my personal trainer.

From victim to master.

Apparently, since I sucked so badly the last time that I threatened him with the use of my gun, he's determined to change this weakness of mine. And at this point, with our bodies standing in such close proximities with one another, the sexual temptation shared between us is as great as ever.

Honestly, I shouldn't feel this nervous around him. After all, he is my husband. Plus, it's not like we're virgins. Although we haven't slept together since I moved in; however, we did spend at least one night together during our marriage. Twelve years ago, right before he left for college.

It was during the summer season, when we first got married and graduated from high school. I had recently been released from the hospital, and was still living at my grandmother's cabin. And on one lazy and sunny day, we were lying outside together in the forest, resting above a bed of white daisies.

At the time, I was staring above at the majestic blue sky and counting the white fluffy clouds passing by. Since childhood, counting clouds was one of my favorite pastimes. And as I stared up at the clouds, Jack gazed up at the same blue sky to admire the birds flying by.

Even back then, he was fascinated by birds— particularly, bluebirds. For the boy who had everything in this world, there was yet one thing that he didn't own: *a bluebird*. Not only was it his upmost desire to catch one, but he also wanted to tame it, too. However, whenever he attempted to capture it, the bird consistently managed to fly away.

In many ways, I, too, felt like I was one of those bluebirds. Both of us creatures, never truly belonged anywhere. Just a flock of visitors, passing through the meadows. Even after my parents died and I moved into my grandmother's cabin, I never viewed my stay in the forest as my permanent residence.

Instead, my intuition always felt that my stay in Portland was only temporary. Eventually, with the passage of the seasons, I knew that I was destined to leave. Like the birds traveling across the blue sky, I, too, was meant to fly away.

Although Jack tried his best to keep me safe within the golden cage, better known as Cerulean Manor; however, my stay at his ancestral home was simply too much to bear. Unfortunately, the abuse that I suffered there was far too great. In fact, just the thought of Vivian Warner right now, makes me shudder with fright.

Even though those days of horror are long gone and behind me, I still don't have the courage to confess about my dark past to Jack. Good or bad, Vivian is still *his mother*. And for an orphan girl who lost her own mother at an early age, I never wanted Jack to think badly of his own mother. In the end, they are still mother and son, bounded by blood.

And so, on that bright and sunny summer day in June, as Jack and I nestled together within the seclusion of the serene forest, our lustful encounter became our first and last time spent together as man and wife.

"Stand still," he whispers into my ear.

Right now, my mind has gone completely blank, and I'm struggling to concentrate on this challenge. Instead, I'm focused on the feel of Jack's body against mine, as he stands right behind me.

Currently, he's leaning in, with his chest pressed up against my back. At this point, I can feel my ass nestled against his thigh. Meanwhile, one of his arms is wrapped around my waist, and the other is resting on my arm. Being the perfectionist that he is, Jack's trying to correct my standing position to better improve my aim.

However, this task is sadly, *failing*. And badly, too.

Instead, right now, at this very second, all I want to do is to throw this revolver down onto the floor, rip off my clothes and sleep with Jack.

Alas, after twelve years of sexless nights, at long last, my body is craving for the touch of a lover!

Moreover, I want Jack!

In all of our years spent apart, I never kept a lover. Not a single one.

I suppose that deep down inside, I really was a faithful wife, after all. And based on what I've read online, I don't think that Jack has been involved with anyone else seriously, either. Hence, shouldn't we just go ahead and give into our desires? To finally have sex, once and for all?

"Jack…," I utter his name aloud, as I take in a breath.

Right now, my heart is beating so fast, and I'm beginning to sweat out of nervousness.

"Yes?" he whispers into my ear, using a very low, deep and seductive voice.

A sexy voice that sends a tremble down my spine. A sultry and hypnotic voice that only Jack owns.

"I don't think I can concentrate, right now," I gulp, as I nervously confess my fears aloud to him.

If I was braver, then I'd ask him for sex, directly. But I'm not going to be the first one to admit this. No, he needs to make the first move. Not me.

"And why not?" he asks me, as he breathes against my neck. "Shall I try to make you feel more comfortable?"

And with those words, his hand dips below my waist and travels down towards my stomach. Before I know it, he's inside my pants, while his hand wanders all the way down towards my underwear.

"Shall I make you feel good?" he teases me.

"Yes," I nod my head, shamelessly.

This is the first time that he's touched me in years. And as his hand begins to play with my folds, I close my eyes shut and release a sigh. It's a good thing that Jack rented out this shooting range today, because apart from us, there's no one else around to witness our naughtiness.

"Ride my fingers, Kayla," he orders, as he inserts two fingers into my womb.

God, it's been forever since I last felt like this! Having him inside of me, fills me with a pleasure that I haven't experienced since my teenage years. Back, when we still lived in the forest.

Slowly, he beings to thrust inside of me, while I ride his fingers. But gradually, Jack increases his speed, and I'm struggling to keep up.

But his fingers alone are not enough. No, I need more of him. *Right now.*

"Take off your pants," I order him in return.

"Oh? Are my fingers not enough for your pleasure? Do you want my cock, too?" he taunts me.

Unfortunately, at this moment, I don't have the patience to deal with a playful Jack. Instead, I want to devour this man, and fuck him hard with all my might. With the gun still held in my hand, I pull myself away from Jack's grip and swiftly spin around to face him.

"Take off your pants, now," I order him, as I hold the gun pointed directly at his heart.

And to my pleasure, Jack happily smiles from ear-to-ear.

"Of course, my little bluebird," he tells me. "Shall I unbuckle my belt, or will you do the honors?"

He's enjoying this. I can tell. His alpine green eyes are glowing as bright as ever. It's filled with curiosity, pleasure and above all else, *wickedness.*

"I'll do it," I agree, as I toss the gun aside, landing straight down onto the ground.

Eagerly, I unbuckle his belt and pull his pants down, exposing his cock instantly. It's thick, hard, and *huge.* God, it's been so long since I last saw it! Honestly, I forgot as to just how big it is, too!

Without thinking any further, I immediately drop down onto the floor and hungrily, I swallow Jack's dick straight into my mouth. My fast reaction also catches him by surprise, as his green eyes widens by my impulsive action.

"God, Kayla!" he roars, as his fingers dig deeply into my loose honey-brown hair.

Carefully, I pull my mouth out and proceed to lick him, starting from his tip and all the way up to his base. Over and over again, I lick and suck him dry, then swallow his cock whole in my mouth. Eventually, he releases his juice and being the greedy girl that I am, I swallow every last drop of him.

"Fuck me, Jack," I demand.

Right now, I might be too forward in this sexual cat and mouse game of ours; but I honestly don't care, anymore. It's been ages since I last had sex with him. And after twelve long years of separation, I'm ready for us to be intimate with one another again.

"With pleasure," Jack tells me, as he swiftly lifts me up to my feet and carries me off to the opposite side of the room.

With my back leaning up against the wall, Jack pulls my pants off and underwear down and tosses them aside onto the floor. A second later, he wraps my legs around his waist and plunges his hips forward. And as he slams his dick right past my inner walls, the impact sends me waves of blissful pleasure upon his entrance.

Meanwhile, as Jack fucks me, I realize two things. One, he's just as equally eager as me to have sex. And two, he's missed me, too.

Thrust after thrust, Jack mercilessly pounds into my swollen flesh, as I claw against his back with my fingernails. Right now, we are like two animals in heat. Fucking one another, as if we're still out in the wild.

The first time we had sex, Jack was a gentle cub. The second time, he's now a heartless beast. From a sweet deer to a ruthless wolf. Oh my, how much the times have changed!

"Faster," I beg him. "I want to feel you even deeper."

My words certainly encourage him. Eager to please me, Jack pumps inside of me, like there's no hope for tomorrow. Acting as if this moment might be our very last day on earth, and he's set on pleasing me until the world ends.

But this position is not enough. Instead, I want to feel him even deeper. And so, I push Jack onto the floor and with his back leaning against the ground, I take full control.

Straddling above him, I lower my body onto him, as I slide his dick right into my wet womb. Upon direct contact, skin-to-skin, we both moan aloud.

"Aaaaahhhhh…," we both utter.

And now, with his cock plunged deep inside of me, I begin to rock back and forth, as I ride him, fiercely.

Meanwhile, as I thrust above him, acting like a cowgirl riding a bull in a rodeo, Jack fondles with my jiggling breasts. Leaning his head up, he begins to lick and suck on my right nipple, as his other hand flicks the other.

"Oh God!" I shout, as I bite my lower lip.

The feel of his touch is electrifying. I honestly can't take it. It feels so damn good!

"Take me from the behind," I order him.

Determined to please me, he promptly takes control and flips me over. With my ass facing him, he plunges his dick into my behind. Meanwhile, his hands are cupping my breasts from the floor, as his cock rapidly moves within me.

The excitement I feel is like no other, and I don't want this moment to end. Whatever the future holds for us, I'll take it. If being with him brings this much pleasure to my body, then so be it. I'll remain as Mrs. Warner, if it means that I can feel his dick inside of me, every single day for the rest of our lives.

"Come for me," he orders, as he moves deeper inside of me.

At this point, I'm about ready. My mind, body and soul are all on a speeding rollercoaster. Today's lesson might have started out as a practice run around the shooting range; but one way or another, this hunter has finally caught his lost bird.

And with that last and final thrust, I finally come and scream his name as loud as I possibly can.

"Jack!!!" I yell at the top of my lungs, before collapsing down onto the floor.

Afterwards, for the rest of the afternoon, I rest comfortably against Jack's warm chest. And after twelve long years, my husband finally has me all to himself.

51

CHAPTER 7

Monte Carlo

After a fourteen-hour flight, Jack and I land at the airport in Monte Carlo. According to Jack, this trip is meant to secure a new business venture for his administration by partnering with a few notable businessmen from Monaco.

In particular, my husband is scheduled to meet this afternoon with the billionaire entrepreneur and tycoon, Logan Redding, aboard his private yacht. According to Jack, Logan owns a successful tech company called Viper, which specializes on building high tech internet infrastructures and cloud computing software for various private industries and governments.

Currently, the state government as a whole, is still operating using twentieth century technology. Unlike most governments around the globe, the golden state still hasn't reached its potential on fully transitioning into the digital era.

As the new Senator of California, Jack desires to modernize the state by establishing an e-government service, which will allow citizens to interact with their local governments through an online system. In translation, this means people can register their cars, change their addresses, pay their parking fees, university fees and every other state fee— all completed through a central online database.

Furthermore, Jack also wants to secure the means to rebuild the state's crumbling transportation infrastructure, including renovating several major metropolitan airports, roads, buses, trains and driverless cars. Therefore, by securing a deal with Logan, Jack will be able to use his cloud hosting services to modernize California, while also networking with other tech gurus who are a part of Logan's orbit.

Furthermore, ever since my debut at the black and white tie charity ball, Jack also secured a deal with Katherine Petruchio's husband, James, who owns a tech business of his own called Verona, which specializes on producing AI chips. With these chips, Jack can incorporate these new and emerging technologies towards his goal on fostering new smart cities of the future.

As for my reasons for attending this trip… well… there are mainly three reasons. First, as Jack's wife, having me by his side serves as a good form of PR. My appearance on this trip further promotes the image that he and I are on a united front, with me serving as his ever dedicated and dutiful wife.

Second, and perhaps the most interesting fact above all else, Jack wants me to spy for him. While he's busy entertaining the men, my role is to mingle with their wives or girlfriends, and gather as much intelligence as I possibly can. Who knew that all of my etiquette lessons with Evelyn would come in so handy, after all!

Third, since our last erotic encounter at the shooting range, Jack and I have been inseparable. No longer do we maintain separate bedrooms. Instead, after that day, once I stepped back into our home, I quickly packed up my belongings and moved them over into Jack's bedroom.

Since then, I haven't slept anywhere else other than his bed. But in truth, at night, we hardly sleep. Instead, it's been a nonstop wild sex marathon, each and every night. Truly, it's a miracle that I'm not already pregnant!

And now that we've landed in Monte Carlo, I'm ready to start my mission. To do so, I'll be meeting with my new acquaintances at the local café. Meanwhile, Jack will be busy sailing around the harbor with Logan. Hopefully, we can both take advantage of this trip and get some things done!

CHAPTER 8

Casino Royale

Tonight, Casino Royale, the world's most famous casino that's located in the heart of downtown Monte Carlo, is as glamorous as ever. Since arriving to the lobby about twenty minutes ago, I've been busy admiring all of the guests. Many of whom, are famous celebrities, businessmen and political figures that I recognize from the magazines.

From sequin, shiny and bright gowns worn by the ladies, with their high-end Louis Vuitton purses and Christian Louboutin heels, along with the men dressed in their finest suits, ties, cufflinks and wingtip oxford shoes, the world of glamour and luxury dominates tonight's atmosphere.

As for Jack and I, we came dressed up to play our parts, too. As a power couple, we're a perfect match. Together, we arrived both dressed in the color black. Him in a black Armani silk suit, while I'm dressed in a black sequin mermaid style Versace gown. Meanwhile, his tie and three-point pocket square are cobalt blue, purposely selected to match my sapphire and diamond necklace, earrings and eyes.

With my long hair swept aside and secured in a tight ponytail that dangles across my back in the form of thick waves of curls; for the first time in ages, my normally tangled mess of a hair is finely tamed and ready to mingle. Additionally, smokey navy blue eyeshadow has been smudged across my eyelids, while a thick layer of mascara has been applied over my lashes. And lastly, to top it all off, a generous layer of nude lip gloss has also been painted over my lips.

As it turns out, my afternoon session of high tea with the ladies wasn't so eventful, after all. As much as Jack wanted me to spy on them, the truth is that there really wasn't any intel to gather on the wives or girlfriends to his business associates at all.

In reality, most of these wealthy women are simply preoccupied with either the latest high fashion currently dominating the runway or their ongoing charity works. To be perfectly fair, I wouldn't call them all entirely shallow. Unfortunately, their superficial bubbles are all they know. In truth, most of these women have either been born wealthy or married into it. Sadly, they've never actually experienced a world, in which they were an active member of a typical American working-class family.

Luckily, for me, I still haven't fully transitioned into their mindsets and in truth, I don't think I ever will. Like them, I might have married into wealth myself; however, I haven't forgotten about my roots, either.

Growing up in the woods, it taught me to be humble. Furthermore, for the past twelve years, living as a single and struggling entrepreneur, I've learned firsthand that wealth truly comes and goes. Like a traveling gust of wind, wealth is only temporary.

Moreover, after my failure on gathering intel during my teatime with the ladies, I'm starting to think that Jack secretly asked me to spy on these women just as an excuse for me to mingle with other ladies within our social circle. To make new friends, as he so often and eloquently suggests that I do.

Granted, in the past, I might have been shy, with my only

friends being Rebecca and Mrs. Wong; but still, I'm picky. I like to keep my social circle small and safe. However, given that I'm married to a public figure now, I don't think that I can keep my world small anymore. Instead, like a bird, the time has come for me to stretch my wings and grow. To finally, expand my horizon.

However, tonight, might be more eventful than my time spent at the café this afternoon. Because right now, we're off to the roulette table!

Like the spy movies, I'm here as Jack's official date. After securing his deal with Logan earlier this afternoon; tonight, Jack is going to meet with a few more potential investors. And so, if Jack can make a good impression on them, then he might be able to land another impressive deal.

But these men are no ordinary businessmen. According to Jack, they're also notorious gamblers. Men, who not only possesses wealth beyond measure, but also prefers making deals over a game of roulette. To them, they'll take a roulette table any day, over negotiating a business deal at a conference table.

In reality, these spoiled men are real bastards. Against their own better reasonings, they prefer luck over logic. A reflection of the true spoils of undeserving wealth.

And so, we're forced to play by their game. With Jack playing the part of the suave and debonair gambler; and I, as his good luck charm.

Currently, we're seated at a roulette table, near the front entrance of the casino. Across from us, sits Evan Saintclaire, an elderly billionaire in his seventies, twice divorced and now, newly engaged to a much younger woman. Like Logan, he, too, enjoys sailing around the Mediterranean Sea aboard his billion-dollar yacht.

However, what sets Evan apart from Logan, is that he owns a global shipping company, which transports various equipment around the world. Translation: If Jack can secure a deal with him, then Evan's company can transport the raw materials that he needs to build the state's new infrastructure at an affordable price.

Meanwhile, on our left, sits Percy Dumont, another wealthy billionaire entrepreneur. While Evan owns a highly reputable shipping company for commerce, Percy owns the physical raw materials that's needed for the transport. According to Jack, he owns a high supply of steel, which can be used for building future projects involving train tracks, airport terminals, and other transportation needs.

And next to each one of these men, are their women. A blonde for Evan and a brunette for Percy. Both women are dressed in sparkling and revealing gowns, and appears no older than thirty.

As much as playing the part of a good luck charm isn't my forte; however, in support of Jack and his cause, I'm here by his side. Well… technically… I'm not exactly on his side… because I'm actually sitting right on top of his lap!

"If it lands on red, then I'm going to finger you," he seductively whispers into my ear, as his hand rests above my thigh.

Instantly, I shudder at the very thought. Luckily, with Evan, Percy and their partners seated across from us, no one can see what we're actually doing on our end, underneath the table.

"Is that so?" I whisper to my side, challenging him right back.

Meanwhile, as I gaze into his alpine green eyes, I happily watch them light up with pure splendor. My words have enticed him. Based on his reaction, he's excited for sure.

And as the wheel spins around in a circle, Jack's hand slides underneath my slit and travels up my inner thigh. Instantly, I suck in a breath, as his hand rests right along the edges of my lace underwear.

"Are you hoping that it lands on red?" he teases me. "Or do you secretly want it to land on black?"

"Don't you win, if it lands on red?" I ask him.

"I plan on winning, either way," he wickedly grins from ear-to-ear.

"We can make this more exciting," I dare him.

"Ah, is that so?" he raises his brow. "What will you do for me, if the ball lands on red and I win this game?"

Staring across the table, I observe Evan and Percy, along with their dates. Both parties are so lost in the thrill and excitement of the night, that neither seems to care as to whether or not they actually win or lose.

To them, this game is just another form of their nightly entertainment. And instead of paying close attention to a game that's supposed to be related to a business deal, they're currently more preoccupied with making out with their women.

"If it lands on red, then we'll collect your earnings and sign your contracts," I propose to him.

"Afterwards?" he asks me in anticipation.

"Afterwards," I lean into his ear and say, "I'll fuck you mercilessly upstairs in our room, in celebration of your win."

And to Jack's pure joy, the ball lands straight on red.

CHAPTER 9

Sex, Lies & Politics

After Jack collected his winnings and signed his contracts, we rushed upstairs into our hotel bedroom to celebrate our victories.

As much as tonight's outcome is a major win for the state, it's also a win for us, too. Given that Jack won our wager, it's now my turn to deliver his winnings.

"Take off your pants, Mr. Warner," I order him, directly.

I have no time to waste. If I'm going to fuck him, then I want to do it as quickly as possible. To be fair, I haven't slept with Jack, ever since we last boarded a plane out of SFO. And now, my body is desperate for our reunion.

"With pleasure, Mrs. Warner," Jack winks at me, as he proceeds to undress.

Meanwhile, I begin to strip down myself, tossing my sparkling black gown aside and onto the floor. Afterwards, I peel the rest of my undergarments, until I'm left standing stark naked.

"I've decided," Jack tells me, as he takes a step forward, moving away from the shadows. "I know that you're eager to fuck me, but I've got a confession to make."

"Oh?" I ask him, with my raised brow. "Whatever could that be?"

"Turn around, first," he orders, as he reaches for me.

Right now, my knees are hitting the edge of the bed, while his naked body is pressed down on my behind.

"Now, spread your legs apart, so I can come in," Jack whispers into my ear, as he bites down and nibbles on my earlobe.

Instantly, a shiver goes down my back. Originally, I wanted to ride on top of him. However, if he wants to take me from my behind, then so be it!

Following his command, I spread my legs far apart, as my hand grips the edge of the bed. Already, I'm excited. And as soon as I give him an inch of an opening, he swiftly leans in, wraps his arms tightly around my waist and slides his thick cock inside my behind.

"You know," he announces, as he starts to move inside of me, "I got into politics because of you, Kayla."

It's hard to concentrate on his words. Already, my body is heating up, and his penetration is so intense. Thrust after thrust, he's rapidly moving inside of me. Pumping in and out of my behind, while whispering earth shattering words into my ear.

"What do you mean?" I struggle to ask, as I tightly grip the bedsheets with my hands and roughly bite down on my lips.

"You never looked for me," Jack says, as he continues to ram his dick up my womb, fiercely. "And I was tired of waiting. So, I needed to gain your attention."

Suddenly, his words leave me breathless. Was his entire political career really just for me?

"Wait, did you actually run for office, so that I'd come running back to you?" I ask him, dumbfounded. "Politics, embedded within a web of lies? A reason for us to reunite, just so we could have sex again?"

"Don't get me wrong," he answers, shyly, "Sex with you is great. But the truth is… I missed you, Kayla. And I knew that if I got into politics in your home state, then I'd be on television and back in your orbit, again."

His words are both heartwarming and heart-wrenching, all at the same time. In all of our many years spent apart, I never once doubted Jack's sincerity. I always knew that he loved me. Love was never a question when it came to Jack.

But unfortunately, our fates were never aligned and circumstances beyond our control drove us apart. However, hearing that he got into politics, ran and won an entire election just to find me again, touches my heart beyond words.

"Oh, Jack—" I cry out.

"Shush," he interrupts, as he attempts to console me. "You don't have to say anything. Just know, that everything that I did… the election… becoming a senator… Project Bluebird… even this trip… it's all been for *you*. I wanted you back, by any means necessary. And now that I have you, I also want to be a better man for you, too."

His confession is like poetry to my ears. I love this man, through and through. And I don't want another twelve years to go by, without him knowing just how much I love him, too.

That I've always loved him, and I always will.

"I love you, Jack," I finally speak the words that I've waited too long to admit. "Then, *and* now."

My surprising admission shocks and excites him. Instantly, he loses complete control, and his body goes buck wild.

Wrapping his fingers around my honey-brown locks, Jack pulls my hair back as his hips push forward uncontrollably, ramming deeper and harder into my body.

Thrust… after… thrust… harder… faster… deeper… he's pounding my womb like a maniac gone wild, with the slaps of our flesh echoing across the room. Sex with Jack is wild, rough and sexy as hell.

A moment later, we finally reach our climaxes together and collapse forward onto the bed.

Grabbing me from my behind and tightly pressing my naked body against his chest, he tells me, "I love you, Kayla. And I'm never, ever letting you go. From now, until eternity."

And with that vow, I close my eyes and finally accept my fate.

CHAPTER 10

Monster-in-Law

Six months after my reunion with Jack, his mother, Vivian Warner, finally decided to pay us a visit.

She never changed, since the last time I saw her. The same short chin-length platinum blonde hair, with a thick and straight line of bangs. Red painted lips, with matching red nails. A full face of heavy makeup. Wearing another high-end designer made white satin suit with Christian Louboutin heels, along with a leather handbag that's probably worth thousands of dollars. A purse that's most likely, worth more in value than my entire flower shop and apartment combined.

But, apart from a few wrinkles around the edges of her eyes and along the far corners of her mouth, Vivian still resembles the same woman, whom I remember back from twelve years ago. And that alone, terrifies me to my core.

For over a decade, this woman has haunted my dreams. Many times, I've woken up in the middle of the night just shaking in fear. Sadly, in the dark, I'm left recalling the past horrors of abuse, which I previously suffered under her watch.

And now, after desperately trying to escape from her wrath,

here I am, facing my abuser, once again. Seeing the face of the devil, whom I sought so hard to run away from all those many years ago.

"It's good to see you again, Kayla," she casually tells me over dinner.

Of course, I know that this is a *lie*.

Vivian is *not* happy to see me. Her face says it all.

Although she might have a blanket expression covering her; however, I can see right through her veil. She's as cold as ice.

If this was a fairy tale, then she'd be the villainous, Ice Queen. A villainess queen, who's still clearly displeased that I, a mere peasant, am the bride of her one and only darling son.

"Yes, it's good to have Kayla at home," Jack beams with pride, as he takes a sip of his red wine. "Back at my side, where she belongs."

"Interesting," Vivian notes, as she cuts through her bloody meat with a sharpened steak knife.

A knife that she probably, secretly wants to use against *me*. Thank goodness, Jack is here besides me in this very room!

"So, Kayla, how long are you planning to stay here?" she asks me, directly.

Her stare is so intense. Her russet brown eyes are practically penetrating right through my very soul. If ever there was the gaze of death, then the Grim Reaper has some competition with the likes of Vivian Warner.

"Forever," Jack interjects on my behalf. "Kayla is my wife. Where I go, she shall follow me."

"But that wasn't always the case," Vivian kindly reminds us, as her red lips curves upwards into a perfect smile. "Are we all forgetting about the past? After all, Kayla does have a tendency to run away. She's like a wandering little bluebird, with no boundaries or attachments."

"I… I… I…," I struggle to find the words to respond to her accusation.

Luckily, much to my relief, Jack intervenes on my behalf. Gently, he places his hands above mine, which are currently resting above my lap and underneath the table. With his alpine green eyes narrowed and shining brightly, he addresses his mother, sternly.

"That's enough," he speaks, with his voice as cold as ice.

A chill that's equal to the ice queen seated across from me at the table.

"The past is behind us," he tells her calmly and confidently. "All that matters now, is that Kayla is *my wife*. Moving forward, we plan to live our lives together, as a normal married couple."

"Well," Vivian huffs in disagreement, "If that's your wish, then, who am I to question your union? Do as you please."

"Good, I'm glad that we've finally reached an understanding," Jack grins, as he stares at his mother with the look of a madman.

Cutting straight through the heart of his beef with his steak knife, Jack gazes at his mother, while he devours the rest of his meal. Secretly, he's sending her an unspoken message not to mess with me. A threat, soaked in blood.

However, the truth is that I'm still in the dark, when it comes to Jack's relationship with his mother. Although Vivian appears to be the loving, devoted and adoring mother; however, after witnessing their shared interaction tonight, I'm not entirely certain if he's an equally loving, devoted and adoring son to her, in return.

But either way, with Jack's unlimited support, I finally have the confidence that I need to remain within Vivian's company.

And so, with him safely by my side, I comfortably eat the rest of my meal in peace.

An hour later, Jack, Vivian and I are lounging away in the parlor. While Jack is smoking a Cuban cigar, I'm quietly seated on the sofa and enjoying a warm cup of black coffee. Meanwhile, Vivian is seated across from me on a reading chair, and is currently reviewing today's newspaper.

"Jack, have you seen the latest headline about Kayla?" she directly asks her son.

Rather than addressing *me*, the subject at hand; Vivian, clearly makes it a point to ignore my presence in the room, altogether.

"No, I haven't, as I don't read anything that comes from the press. It's all garbage," Jack replies, as he inhales his cigar and then, releases a ring of smoke from out of his mouth.

"Garbage or not, it does concern Kayla," she informs him.

And then glancing at my direction, she finally acknowledges me and with a wicked grin, she says, "Kayla, I apologize in advance; but we really can't ignore this article."

Whatever it is that Vivian is so eager to share with us tonight, I can already tell that this isn't good news. Plus, given the fact that Vivian decided to bring up this matter so soon after dinner, then she must have some hidden ulterior motive as well.

"If it's not kind words about Kayla, then it's not worth mentioning it at all," Jack warns her.

Instantly, I release a breath of relief. Thank goodness that Jack is here to defend me!

"Well, I wouldn't say that this article is entirely terrible, for say," Vivian presses on. "After all, it's only about Kayla's past. It seems that the press has finally gotten a hold of my daughter-in-law's origins."

"Give me that," Jack growls, as he reaches over and snatches the article from out of his mother's hands.

A second later, he quickly tosses the newspaper into the nearest trash bin.

However, from the corner of my eye, I catch the article's title.

From Rags-to-Riches: How the Wild Orphan Gypsy Seduced and Married the Senator.

Alas, my past as an orphan living in a cabin with my grandmother out in the remote woods, has finally caught the ears of the press.

"Kayla, please don't worry," Jack attempts to console me.

Already, he can sense my agitation.

"First thing tomorrow, I'll give Evelyn a call," he reassures me. "She's got plenty of connections with the press. I'm sure that she can straighten out this matter in no time."

Silently, I nod in agreement, while pretending not to be bothered by this disappointing news. However, the truth is that I am bothered. Unfortunately, both in the past and present, part of my insecurities with our relationship is that I never felt that I was good enough to be with Jack. And right now, even as married adults, I still don't want to be a blemish to Jack's perfect career.

Furthermore, as I gaze upon my mother-in-law's face, I can't help but notice the blissful expression resting upon her. Deep down inside, I know that she's most likely responsible for this leak. Because apart from my grandmother, Jack, Evelyn, Rebecca and Mrs. Wong, no one else knows about my past in Portland.

That is, except for Vivian.

And now, with much clarity, I realize that my future with Jack will not be as simple as I had originally hoped it would be. After all these years, the monster from my past has finally returned to reck hell upon my life. A monster with short and platinum blonde hair, and frequently visits the Chanel's and Gucci's runways as their number one client. And that person is none other than...

Vivian Warner, my monster-in-law.

CHAPTER 11

Venus Flytrap

Two days later, I visit Belladonna to check on how my business is faring. After that negative article written about me in the press, Jack and Evelyn quickly squashed the story and instead, had the local newspaper publish a more positive piece about me by focusing on my charity works.

Since reconciling with my husband, I've also subsequently accepted my current position as a political spouse. And, as a political spouse, I've been thrust into a pile of endless paperwork and correspondences— many of which, are a combination of letters authored by the general public, as well as various charities and nonprofit organizations, all inviting me to collaborate with them on several prospective future business ventures.

Furthermore, based upon public feedback, it seems that the media has also most recently bought into the epic and romanticized love story surrounding my marriage. Apparently, our reunion has been so well received by the general public, with many believing that Jack and I are star-crossed lovers.

According to the rumors, while Jack was busy running for office, I was heroically traveling abroad and serving as a devoted former ambassador to the Peace Corps. Apparently, as a Peace Corps Ambassador, I was previously stationed in impoverish neighborhoods located in Eastern Europe and North Africa, respectively.

And now, with me supposedly back from my diplomatic missions, many from the press presume that I will now focus my time on humanitarian projects led by the United Nations.

However, rather than focusing on international issues; instead, I want to apply my charity work here, locally. In fact, since becoming a senator's wife, I've been reviewing Katherine Petruchio's background and have been quite impressed by her overall work.

Apparently, after losing the last election to my husband, Katherine returned back to her old roots and relaunched her former nonprofit and gallery, Bianca & Minola. While her gallery has been a great hit with the local art scene; however, it's her art classes that have truly caught my eye.

As a form of goodwill, Katherine also teaches art lessons to the local community— particularly, classes aimed at developing the youth, who primarily come from underprivileged neighborhoods. Every Wednesday at four o'clock in the afternoon, she hosts landscape lessons to the teens in our city, free of charge. Admiring this positive outlet for our youth, I decided to join in on this venture, too.

As a result, a week ago, I personally reached out to Katherine to properly introduce myself. At first, she was tickled that I, Kayla Warner, was not only the wife of her former political opponent; but that I was also ironically, the florist who served at her own wedding, too. However, being the down-to-earth person that she is, Katherine wasn't at all upset or bothered by my past omission. Instead, she gladly extended her welcoming hand over to me.

Happily, I accepted her warm friendship and partnership. And so, using my grand talents with floral arrangements, I struck a deal with Katherine. Therefore, moving forward, while she continues to host her landscape lessons on Wednesdays; I, in return, will host free floral arrangement lessons on Thursdays at Bianca & Minola for the teens in our community.

For me, these classes serves two purposes. One, it fulfills my public charity work obligation, as one of the primary duties often delegated to a political spouse. And second, it allows me to also give back to my community by doing the one thing that I love most in the world: flowers.

Growing up in the forest, flowers were my entire world. As the granddaughter of an aging retiree, I wasn't able to afford anything of monetary value, like the other girls in my class. Meanwhile, as Jack owned a fine collection of golden figurines kept within the curiosity cabinets at Cerulean Manor; I, on the other hand, possessed only a handful of golden marigolds, recently plucked from the meadow by my own bare hands. A lovely bouquet that was free of charge and was still nevertheless, beautiful.

And so, as flowers became my world, I memorized each and every flower that flourished within the forest. From the cream-colored daises that grew alongside the river to the lavender violets that resided near the far corners of my grandmother's miniature garden, to even the deadly belladonnas that blossomed within the tall and grassy fields. The exquisite yet deadly flower that mostly reminded me of Jack.

Since becoming Kayla Warner, I, too, like a flower, am still trying to blossom into my role as the wife of a senator. Throughout our relationship, there's always been a huge social gap between Jack's world and mine. However, this discrepancy alone isn't enough to hold me back, anymore. This time around, I want to make everything right between us, again. Instead of running away like I did in the past; now, I want to bloom alongside with Jack, as we walk together hand-in-hand into an unknown future.

And so, hosting floral arrangement lessons keeps me close to my roots. By day, I can remain as a proper political spouse by helping my husband with his causes; and by night, I can still be Kayla, the florist. In the end, I don't have to give up either one of my worlds.

But for now, I'm returning back to Belladonna to check on my business. Even though I know that Rebecca is running the operations perfectly; however, I still want to visit my flower shop and collect a few floral arrangements for this week's upcoming class.

However, when I push through the front doors, to my surprise, I notice that the shop is empty. For the first time since opening Belladonna, the store is completely silent.

But there's also something different about Belladonna, too. Staring straight ahead to the far corner of the room, I notice a foreign plant resting above the counter. Walking up towards it, I curiously gaze at the plant and soon realize that it's a Venus Flytrap.

Why is a Venus Flytrap in my shop? I've never carried this plant before. Plus, I highly doubt that Rebecca would ever dare to bring in a new plant, without consulting with me first.

In the past, I always hated Venus Flytraps. As a plant notoriously known for danger, the Venus Flytrap also possesses the ability to destroy things— killing any fly or critter that approaches it. In fact, one summer while visiting a local greenhouse, this plant nearly bit me. Luckily, Jack was nearby to pull me towards safety.

And in many ways, this plant also greatly reminds me of Vivian Warner. Ironically, she, like the plant, always served as a dangerous threat to my safety.

However, as I approach the plant, I also notice a letter left in front of it. Picking it up, I open the envelope and pull out the letter. It states the following:

Kayla Warner,

Get lost, now. Or, else, perish like the flies surrounding this plant.

Signed,

Your Enemy

Instantly, my heart plummets down to my chest. Why would someone write this cruel note to me? For what reason? And whom, exactly, is my enemy?

But before I know it, I notice the shadow of a stranger, reflected against the wall. To my horror, they are standing right behind me.

A second later, a cloth heavily drenched in chloroform is placed over my mouth and then, my entire world immediately goes blank.

CHAPTER 12

Red

"Mr. Warner, you must find her!" Rebecca Fulton desperately begs me, as she frantically shouts at the top of her lungs, while standing in panic and trembling in my office.

Right now, my worst nightmare has tragically come to light. My wife, my beloved Kayla, has been taken from me. Kidnapped, against her will. This very act alone is worthy of my unholy wrath.

For years, I patiently waited for Kayla's return. After everything that we've gone through, I truly believed that at long last, we'd finally have the chance to experience some peace and happiness together. Damn it, how foolish I was to think, otherwise!

As a political figure, Kayla and I are in the public's eye. Unfortunately, as a result, there will always be threats posed against us. However, I presumed that if I assigned enough security to monitor and protect her, then she'd be okay.

Instead, today, I failed her. Disgracing myself, as her overprotective husband. Furthermore, according to my Chief of Staff and right-hand man, Isaac Zeppo, Kayla's assigned bodyguard decided to leave early for his shift, when he saw her visiting her flower shop, Belladonna.

If I had my riffle on hand, then I'd gladly murder that son of a bitch bodyguard of hers in cold blood, right this very second. Pull his nails one by one, then chop his fingers off and shove them up his ass.

Afterwards, I'd skin him alive, before leaving him out for dead in a hot and barren desert, so that the vultures can nibble away on his decomposing flesh. But even then, this overwhelming desire of mine still doesn't amount to enough. No, his punishment and death must be far worse…

However, I can't get too lost in my bloody fantasies. Because right now, Kayla needs me. *I must save her.* Afterwards, all hell will break loose with the bastard who stole her away from me!

Releasing a heavy ring of smoke from my cigar, I revert my attention over to Isaac and with a cruel and cold tone, I ask, "Any leads?"

"We've tracked her down," he tells me, as he bows his head. Already, Isaac senses the inner rage that I'm desperately trying to suppress from within.

As much as I wanted Kayla to feel like she still had her freedom; however, as a responsible husband, I also couldn't allow her to live her life entirely unprotected.

As a result, I never told her the truth about the men that I've assigned to watch over her, around the clock. Not to mention, the tracker that I previously installed on her phone, as well as the second tracker hidden inside of her wedding ring.

What can I say? I need to take all possible precautions. Moreover, judging by Isaac's expression, my efforts must have paid off.

"We've located bluebird," he tells me.

Instantly, my heart steadies a beat. His positive words provides me with the much-needed relief that I so desperately desire.

"Bluebird?" Rebecca sniffs her nose and wipes her tears away with a tissue, as she repeats Isaac's words aloud.

"Umm… it's Mrs. Warner's codename," he informs her.

Keeping Isaac on track with our current conversation at hand, I rest my feet against the edge of my desk and order him, directly, "Speak."

"She's being held in a remote cabin, located in Lake Tahoe," he hesitates. "But…"

"But, what?" I boldly repeat, as I empty my cigar butt into the crystal ashtray located above my desk and then, run my fingers through my blonde head of hair.

"You're not going to like the culprit behind her abduction," Isaac informs me.

"I'm not going to like them, either way," I reply, harshly. "As far as I'm concerned, they're as good as dead."

"Then, who took her?" Rebecca decides to ask Isaac directly, beating me to the punch.

Staring straight into my eyes, he says, "Vivian Warner. Your mother has taken Kayla."

And in that instant, my entire world turns flaming red.

CHAPTER 13

A Cabin in the Woods

"Whatever it is, I'll pay you extra!" I desperately beg my captor.

However, based on his stern reaction, I doubt that he'll take my offer. Unfortunately, my captor possesses a smug and cold expression that's currently resting upon his muscular face.

This stranger is a mountain of a man. At first glance, he appears to be well over six feet and seven inches tall. Strong built. Muscles located everywhere, along with a thick black mustache and beard that's covering his face. Currently, he's dressed in all black, with a silver revolver that's dangling off from his leather belt.

Right now, we're hidden in a remote cabin, located deep in the woods. After collapsing into his arms back at Belladonna, a few hours later, I awoke in the backseat of a car, strapped down and traveling up a mountainous road.

Based on our surroundings, it appears that we've crossed over and into the Sierra Nevada Mountains. Plus, judging by the lake view, which I previously saw from outside of the car window, I think that we're mostly likely near Lake Tahoe— a place located about three hours or so outside of San Francisco by car.

To my upmost fear, I don't know a single soul out here. God, I hope that Jack can find me soon. But either way, I can't afford to wait for help. If I'm to survive this ordeal, then I need to strategize and save myself.

"I'm a wealthy woman," I boldly announce to my captor.

To my benefit, he didn't tape my mouth shut. Instead, I'm tied down to a wooden chair, with my hands held behind my back, and my legs strapped to the bottom of my seat. Furthermore, I'm positioned by a brick fireplace, which has a blazing fire burning at the moment.

Quickly scanning around the space, I notice that our cabin appears to be relatively small. Based on my brief observation, there appears to be several tall windows surrounding the premise, along with a few rooms located in the back. If I can somehow secretly untie myself without him noticing, then I can attempt to flee from out of one of these windows.

"My employer has more money than you," he sneers with disdain, as he takes a sip of his cold beer.

"I can top them," I retort. "I'll double it. Just name your price."

At this point, I'd trade my entire life savings, apartment and flower shop, if it means that I can escape from this prison. Whatever it takes, I'm willing to negotiate my freedom in exchange for anything that this man might desire.

"Money, cars, property, you name it," I implore him. "I'll give you anything that you want. Just please, let me go."

"Everything you own, already belongs to my employer," he laughs mockingly, as he quickly chugs down his beer.

His words leave me bewildered. What does he mean by this odd statement? How can his employer own my wealth? Only my husband and I share our wealth. Us, with the exception of…

And then, suddenly, it all becomes so clear. Because at this very moment, my answer soon comes to light, as a familiar female steps forward from out of the shadows, with her short and platinum blonde hair shining brightly against the sunlight that's peeking through the windows. Meanwhile, the click clacking sounds of her signature Christian Louboutin heels are echoing across the room.

Lo and behold, my enemy is finally revealed. And in no surprise, it's my mother-in-law.

Vivian Warner, the root of my demise.

CHAPTER 14

Belladonna

"Kayla, are my eyes playing tricks on me, or are you not too surprised to see me?" Vivian wickedly smiles at my direction, as she enters into the room.

"But then again," my mother-in-law continues on, as she pulls a seat near her henchman. "You were always a clever girl. If only you weren't involved with my son, then I might have liked you. But then again, neither of us can change the past."

Rising up from her chair, Vivian walks over to my side, leans in and whispers into my ear, "You should have kept up with your side of the bargain. You took the money. Remember? Why did you return?"

"Jack wanted me back," I whisper aloud, as I boldly lock direct eye contact with her.

Suddenly, my unprecedented response catches her by surprise. Based on her foul expression, she's clearly displeased by my answer. And as a direct result, her russet brown eyes are gleaming with rage.

"I know," she hisses in anger. "That damn boy was always obsessed with you! You two should have been enemies, not lovers!"

Out of frustration, Vivian raises her hand up in the air and moves to slap my face, with her hand landing on top of my right cheek, smacking it *hard*. Instantly, I flinch. Upon impact, my face is now bright red and throbbing in excruciating pain.

"Kayla Steuber, you are nothing but scum and filth!" she screams, as her sharpened red nails claws against the leather to her seat.

"You're nobody! Nothing else, but a gutter rat! A dirty whore from the slums!" Vivian yells loudly. "You are and have always been unworthy of my son! To think, that *you* of all people, should dare to carry the Warner name!"

"I won't apologize for loving your son," I say with much pride, as I spit a salvia of blood from out of my mouth and watch as it lands across the floor.

After all of these painful years, I never once stood up for Jack. Like a coward, I allowed Vivian to bully and scare me away, in order to avoid pursuing a meaningful relationship with the man, whom I've loved since childhood.

Foolishly, I allowed myself to believe that I was never worthy of his affections. Even though I pushed Jack away for years, he still patiently waited for me. And when I eventually returned back to him, he happily welcomed me with open arms. Never once, questioning me. Instead, only accepting me for the woman that I am.

And now, even in the face of fear, with my life on the line, I'm finally ready to stand up to my oppressor. Whether I live or die, out here in the wilderness, I refuse to die as a coward. I owe it to myself and Jack to defend our love.

"I take back what I said earlier," Vivian gazes at me with intense hate. "You're not clever. On the contrary, you're a stupid girl, after all."

"If loving your son makes me stupid, then so be it," I proudly declare, with my chin held up high.

I might be playing with fire, but I don't care anymore. Against my own will and better judgment, I've been beaten by this woman countless times over, already in my life. If she finally beats me to death, then at least I will have the last laugh in my untimely death.

"You could have lived a long and happy life, if only you had stayed in your lane," she clicks her tongue with displeasure. "Instead, you got greedy. You wanted to be the wife of a senator. Don't think that I didn't catch on to your timing, Kayla. Gone for twelve years, only to reemerge after Jack won the election."

"That's not true!" I exclaim. "Our paths just didn't cross, until then."

"Save your excuses," she rolls her eyes at me. "It doesn't matter, anymore. Either way, I plan to eliminate you."

Walking over to the opposite side of the room, Vivian takes another seat and stretches her arms across the red velvet sofa.

"By the way, I was the one, who leaked your origin story to the press," she mocks me, with a playful grin. "Honestly, I thought that would be enough to scare you away. But I guess I was wrong, after all."

"*You* leaked my story?" I choke.

Even though I know that Vivian hates me and was likely the culprit behind my most recent scandal; however, hearing the truth spoken directly from her own two lips is devastating. Foolishly, I always assumed that she'd keep my past private for the sake of her son and the Warner name. To conceal the very fact that her son had married a lonely and poor orphan girl from the woods.

"Don't look at me like that," she huffs in annoyance. "I needed to do *something*. It's not like I could serve you tea infused with belladonnas again, like I used to do back at Cerulean Manor. If I couldn't poison you like I did before, then I needed to find some other means."

"Kidnapping?" I raise my brow, challenging her to the bitter end.

"Kidnapping… borrowing… call it what you will," she laughs on.

Snapping her fingers together, Vivian sternly orders her henchman to take care of business— aka, me!

With my eyes shut, I'm ready to accept my fate. For twelve long years, I sought hard to flee from the grasp of Vivian Warner. Sacrificing my own marriage and happiness for the sake of this woman.

Tragically, in the end, I still lost and Vivian has finally won.

But, just as I expect to listen to a gunshot being released out into the air; instead, to my surprise, I hear the doors slam right open.

One way or another, Jack has come to my rescue. And to my upmost relief, he's standing here in-person, right in the nick of time.

CHAPTER 15

Justice for Kayla

"It's over Vivian," Jack announces loudly, as he bursts through the front doors of the cabin, along with an armed squat team standing behind him.

Like a real-life hero, Jack arrives right on time. Almost immediately, I release a huge sigh of relief; grateful in the miraculous fact that my husband has literally just saved me from the brinks of death.

Without a further delay, Vivian's henchman is captured by at least five police officers and quickly escorted out of the cabin in handcuffs.

However, the real matter at hand, is the showdown currently going down between my husband and his mother.

"Jack, this is all a misunderstanding," Vivian frantically pleads.

Ever since I've known her, this is the very first time that I've witnessed the sheer look of panic flashing across my mother-in-law's face. Vivian Warner might be a clever and conniving woman, but even she has her limits. At this point, it might be an impossible scenario for her to talk her way out of this crisis.

"Save it, Vivian," Jack stops her. "I heard everything. And…"

Taking a step forward, he comes face-to-face with his mother. With the most sinister expression resting upon my husband's face… an expression, that even, I, as his wife, have never witnessed before on him… from the corner of the room, I silently watch on as Jack proceeds to slap his own mother across her face.

"This is for Kayla," he yells, violently, with his face burning bright red with rage.

"And this," he continues on, as he throws a second slap across her other cheek, "Is for *my mother.*"

Wait.. hold on. My mother? Did Jack just say *his mother?* Why? Isn't Vivian his mother? Am I missing something here?

Unfortunately, before I'm able to hear an answer to this riddle, Vivian is arrested and taken directly into custody by the police. A second later, Jack rushes over to my side and swiftly moves to untie me.

"Kayla, are you alright?" he frantically asks, as he smothers me with kisses and holds me tightly against his chest.

"I am," I nod my head. "Thank God, you came in time."

"Kayla," he gazes deeply into my eyes, while he gently holds my face within the palms of his hands.

"I'm sorry for everything," he apologizes to me, as he bows his head down in shame.

"It's not your fault—"

"No, it is *my fault,*" Jack disagrees. "My first mistake was leaving you behind at Cerulean Manor."

"But Jack, you didn't know," I tell him, as my eyes grow teary. "I never told you about what happened between your mother and I."

Taking in a deep breath, I struggle with my words as I attempt to tell him the truth.

"I.. I… I just didn't have the heart," I studder. "I didn't want you to resent or hate your own mother."

"She's *not* my mother," he growls, angrily. "My biological mother, Judith Warner, died when I was a child. Vivian was my *stepmother.*"

"Your stepmother?" I repeat, in surprise.

Is that what Jack meant, when he slapped Vivian for a second time? Was that act alone, in honor of his late mother?

"I could never prove it before, but that woman murdered my mother," he confesses to me, with deep sadness. "At the time, everyone believed that my mother committed suicide by poisoning herself with tea infused with belladonnas. But, even as a child, I always suspected foul play. Unfortunately, I caught my father having an affair with Vivian, out in the gardens of our estate. And so, in my heart, I knew that Vivian was the culprit, who was responsible for my mother's untimely death. Back then, she was obsessed with marrying my father and becoming the next Mrs. Warner. But fortunately, tonight, after hearing her confession about tampering with your tea, I can now, finally hold her accountable for my mother's death, too."

His confession is heart-wrenching. Not only did I suffer by the hands of Vivian Warner, but so did Judith Warner, too. Hearing that I wasn't Vivian's only victim, only brings further sadness to my heart. Especially, my sadness for Jack. To lose his mother at such a young age, is so incredibly unfair.

"Oh, Jack, I'm so sorry," I attempt to console my husband, as I reach over and embrace him.

"Don't be," he says, as he cradles me within his loving arms. "I'm the one who is sorry. But Kayla, I never intended to leave you at Cerulean Manor, forever. It was only temporarily. At the time, you were still too sick to move. I couldn't risk you traveling to the east coast and relapsing, so soon after your hospital release. However, once the semester was over, I was planning to return and bring you back with me. But by then, you were already gone. And the rest, is well, history."

"So many misunderstandings and unnecessary mistakes made in our past," I sigh aloud, as I somberly reflect. "If only I had been honest with you, from the very beginning."

"Don't blame yourself," he lifts my chin up within the palm of his hand. "We both equally made mistakes, too."

"Then, let's start over," I suggest to him. "Let the past stay in the past. All that matters now is our future together."

"Yes, and now that I've got you, I'm never letting you go."

With that heartfelt promise, Jack kisses me, passionately. Kisses that are ultimately, rooted in love, admiration and affection.

And for the mischievous and beautiful boy who gifted me with my first kiss back in the woods, I realize that he's also the last man on earth, whom I also want to share my last kiss with on my dying day.

Jack Warner.
My lover.
My former enemy.
My best friend.
My husband.
My soulmate.

CHAPTER 16

Happily Ever After

"Mr. Warner, is it true that your stepmother, Vivian Warner, is responsible for the crimes, concerning the kidnapping of your wife and the murder of your biological mother?" asks a male reporter from the *San Francisco Chronicle*.

Right now, Jack and I are up on stage, seated behind a conference table and addressing the press about the latest scandal surrounding my kidnapping. Ever since Vivian's arrest back at Lake Tahoe made headline news, the truth about her past crimes have also resurfaced and have been finally brought to light.

"Yes, it's all true," Jack speaks into the microphone, appearing as confident and as poised as ever.

Currently, he's dressed up in sharp Versace jet black cashmere suit, with an ivory silk tie, which matches my own vintage Chanel ivory tweed dress suit. Together, we are united as a team. Ready to handle the press, as a power couple.

"Vivian Warner is responsible for my wife's kidnapping, as well as the death of my late mother, Judith Warner," he announces to the crowd.

After recently discovering a portrait of Judith Warner hidden within the back end of Jack's desk drawer, instantly, I recognized the resemblance. The same natural blonde hair. Sharp facial features. *Alpine green eyes.*

It was only later on, that Jack explained the truth about his family to me. As it turns out, Vivian is originally a brunette. Idolizing her own childhood friend, Vivian only dyed her hair platinum blonde to copy Judith. According to Jack, his stepmother tried to replicate his biological mother in every possible way. Same hair. Clothes. *Husband.*

However, Vivian's russet brown eyes were always a dead giveaway that she wasn't his true biological mother. And due to her ommetaphobia, she couldn't conceal her eye color with the use of colored contact lenses.

In the end, no matter how hard she tried, Vivian could never truly replace Judith. Especially, in the eyes of Jack— a son who simply refused to erase the loving memories of his late mother.

"As such, my stepmother will be put on trial for her crimes against my late mother," he continues on. "As well as her most recent crime, imposed against my wife."

Suddenly, the flashes of camera lights rapidly increases and the press goes wild. Finally, at long last, it's now my turn to speak.

"Thank you all, for your concerns," I address the crowd. "Luckily, thanks to the relentless efforts and dedication posed by my husband and the entire San Francisco Police Department, I was rescued right on time, safe and unharmed."

"Is it true that Vivian Warner wanted you dead, because of your nomadic past?" asks another reporter. "According to our sources, she believed that your impoverish background made you an unworthy spouse to our senator."

Gently placing his hands on top of mine, Jack answers the question on my behalf.

"My wife is not the unworthy partner in this relationship," he smiles brightly. "It is *I*, who's unworthy for *her*."

"Let it be known to all, that I'm madly in love my wife," he announces, loudly. "Kayla, is my entire world. And if anyone has a problem with her and our relationship, then they have a problem with *me*. I'd sooner give up my seat as a senator, than to ever allow Kayla to leave my side. Now, and forever."

Leaning in, Jack kisses me in front of the entire crowd and the very next day, we make the front cover of the newspaper with the article entitled:

Happily Ever After.

EPILOGUE

Three Years Later

After working hard around the clock, Jack and I, along with our little family, are taking some much-needed time off to enjoy a trip to the countryside.

Since our last press conference held three years after my kidnapping incident, I soon thereafter, discovered that I was pregnant with our first child. Now, three years later, I'm a mother to two children: a two-year-old daughter named, Isabella; and a one-year-old son, named, Beau.

After intense public scrutiny, Jack's father, Sylas, eventually divorced Vivian, leaving her cold and dry to face her crimes, alone. Unfortunately, for her, the evidence in Vivian's trial was so overwhelming that her lawyers were unable to win her case.

As a result, she was found guilty for all of her crimes concerning Judith and myself, and sentenced to a life in prison. Furthermore, her henchman, Gustaf Gibson, was also convicted for his crimes as well. However, unlike Vivian, Gustaf was sentenced to twenty years in prison for his role in my kidnapping.

As for Jack and myself, my husband continues to serve as the

Senator of California, working hard to make our state a better place. Additionally, given his love for his job, he's decided to run for next year's reelection. In the end, Jack's accidental political career actually became his true calling.

Meanwhile, I've been busy, too. Apart from being a wife and a mother, who's raising two young children, I continue to teach my floral arrangement classes at Bianca & Minola, while Rebecca runs Belladonna as the store manager.

Additionally, I've also taken up a few public landscaping projects on the side as well. Primarily, I've been focused on renovating old and abandoned city parks throughout the state and reconverting them into botanical gardens for the local communities to enjoy.

And for today's trip, we're visiting one of my newly remodeled gardens. A botanical garden located out in Sonoma Valley, which is just a short car ride north from San Francisco.

"Isn't the garden beautiful?" I ask Jack, as I let the kids run wild through the garden.

Witnessing my children happily frolicking through the grassy fields, while enjoying the wild garden so freely, brings an unexpected joy to my heart. Even though they're city kids, they still seem to cherish the outdoors. One way or another, Isabella and Beau have somehow managed to inherit my love for nature.

"The garden is as beautiful as my wife," Jack proudly beams, as he places a tender kiss upon my lips.

Together, we gaze across at the sunset, hand-in-hand. Much to my pleasure, the view is spectacular. With the colors of bright blue, burnt orange and pinkish yellow stretching across the majestic sky, Jack and I remain standing in a field of lavender, as monarch butterflies and bluebirds surround us. And as my children laugh and play along the grassy fields, I happily smile on.

In the end, I got the best of both worlds. A loving husband and family. Kayla Warner is no longer the lonely orphan from the woods. Instead, I'm a happy wife and mother. And I wouldn't trade my world for anything else.

The End.

SNEAK PREVIEW #1:

Wake Up, Darling

CHAPTER 1

Once Upon a Coma…

With the sun flashing across my face, I struggle to adjust my eyes. But in truth, I can't *open* them, even if I wanted to. But it's not limited to just my eyes. It's also me moving my hands, too. And my legs. And my feet. And my toes. And my arms. And my fingers. It's *everything*. It's my entire body all at once, because I'm *paralyzed*.

Sadly, it took me a long time to come to this conclusion. But lo and behold, I am, indeed, paralyzed. In fact, I'm currently in a deep coma and everyone around me assumes the worst. That I'm lying on death's door. That in a matter of days… *no*… *hours*… and I'll most likely be declared as dead. Except I'm not. I'm *not* dead. I'm still here!

Strangely enough, I can hear them, but they *can't* hear me. I listen to their loud chatters and gentle whispers. I hear the doctors and the nurses coming in and out, all checking on me periodically. And they've been gossiping about me, too.

Whether I want to or not, I do hear their worries. How tragic my life must have been, according to them. That, for a young woman of thirty years of age, to be in the current vegetative state that I'm in. To be married to a wealthy senator and yet, for all the money in the world, I still lie unconscious in this bed. Even as a world-famous romance author, I, myself, could never have written such a tragic tale. And yet…

There was an accident. An accident that I can't seem to remember, no matter how much I struggle to recall. Something happened to me and whatever it was, it brought me here. To this very hospital. And now, as I lie in this bed, alone with only my silent thoughts and the sounds of my environment, I'm left wondering one question: why didn't I die?

For some reason, God spared my life. Even with all of the morphine pumping into my body to help me heal, I still can't recall what brought me here… and that alone makes me feel so upset.

No, upset isn't the right word. Instead, I'm *angry*. Better yet, I'm *furious*. I'm furious, because while the world perceives me to be in a coma, I'm still wide awake. Or at least, awake on the inside. Awake and silently listening to my surroundings. Hearing both the good and the bad, all around me.

My main visitors have primarily been the nurses. Mainly females. They cry for me. Many of them were my fans, who previously read all of my romance novels. I can hear their cries, and their well wishes. I know that they all mean well. And truly, I am grateful that my novels have brought them much joy and comfort. That, should I die right here, today; then at least my novels will continue to live on. Some piece of my legacy to pass on into the future. A future absent of any children of my own. *An unfinished life.*

Although I'm aware that I'm indeed, married; but in truth, I can hardly remember my husband. He's like a blackened blur. Both him and his face. But regardless, I do know that he *exists*. I can hear the nurses speak of him, time to time. From what I've gathered, he's a senator.

Wealthy, young and handsome.

But has he come to visit me, as of lately? I'm not entirely sure.

However, there's been one man, who's the exception. In fact, he visits me quite often. I can hear him, always weeping. Grieving. His cries of despair might be soft and silent, but I do feel his tear droplets whenever they land upon my face. In truth, it's one of the few exceptions that I can actually *feel* against my entire body. *His endless tears.*

Whenever he enters into my room, the nurses all leave. Often times, he pulls a chair by my bedside and holds my hand. Surprisingly, I can *feel* his touch. It feels warm, nice and safe. But the only problem is that I *can't* move my hand to embrace his, in return. Oh, how I wish that I could! Not being able to touch him, truly feels like hell on earth! It's so unfair and cruel! Oh, how fate cursed me so!

Apart from holding my hand, he doesn't speak much. Honestly, he really doesn't need to. It's not like I can carry a conversation with him, anyways. But either way, he sits there. Silently. Peacefully. Sometimes for only a few short minutes and other times, for several hours on end.

Is he, my husband? I'm not entirely sure. He must be, right? Who else would bother to sit by my constant side, if not for him?

But whomever he is, he does bring me great comfort. Whether he's death or my husband, I don't care. But I do crave his touch. His attention. His affection. I relish on his surprise visits, whenever he comes. And when he's gone, I'm saddened by his absence. Even though I can't speak or touch him, I still *miss* him.

Sometimes, when I'm alone, I often wonder about him. Specifically, of what he looks like. I must have known him in my past. I must have. But then again, my memories are very limited.

Apart from my childhood, career and marital status, everything else is a darkened blur. And if it wasn't for the nurses' gossiping around me, then I'd have never have known that I'm married or that my husband is a senator. Sadly, I suppose this accident of mine really did destroy my memories after all…

Again, when my stranger is gone, I genuinely miss him. Even into the late hours of the night, I continue to fantasize about his appearance. Tall or short? Muscular or chubby? Blonde or brunette? Blue eyes or brown? A doctor or a scholar? A businessman or another senator? My husband or someone… *else?*

Mystery, after mystery, after mystery. Whomever my stranger is, I am forever grateful to him. I'm grateful, because apart from the hospital's medical staff, he's the only other person who continues to visit me on a regular basis. He's the only one holding my hand. The only person who encourages me. Motivates me. *Cries for me.*

Again, he doesn't speak much. But there's one phrase that he always utters. Over and over… and over again…

Wake up…

Wake up…

Wake up…

Wake up… *darling…*

His words are spoken like a prayer. He wishes for me to awaken from this coma and to be fair, I do, too. If only to catch a glimpse of his face.

But the truth is, I am awake. *Wide awake.* It's just that my body isn't. My eyes refuse to open, even though I want it to… oh, so desperately! But even when I command it to do so, it still doesn't obey. One way or another, my own body refuses to listen to me... it's like a violent war raging inside of me... and I'm struggling to win this battle…

But apart from my own internal struggles, his voice remains buried in my mind, as my constant motivation. The way he says the word *darling*, it's so touching. It's uttered, using a sweet and tender melody. Like that special word is just for *me*. A private word shared only between him and myself. That my name might be Karly Summers, but to him, I'm his one and only...

DDDDaaaarrrlllliiinnnggg...

He stretches the vowels and elongates the consonants of this special word, all from the tip of his tongue. He wants me to awaken. So desperately. I can feel it by the sounds of his deep voice. He's trying to enchant me. To encourage me. Anything to have me wake up from this God forsaken coma!

And his words do encourage me. I try. Each day, I try to open my eyes. I practice using every ounce and fiber of my muscles. And one day, I know that I'm going to win this battle. I am going to wake up from this death sentence. I am going to recover. I will overcome my own weakened body, by the sheer power of my mind. I am determined to succeed. I am not a failure, but a fighter. And one day soon, I will open my eyes and rise again!

Because I've decided that this stranger is not death, but my savior. An angel who is desperately trying to keep me here on this earth. To stay alive. To recover. To reunite back with him. To simply *be with him*.

And so, for the next few days, I concentrate. I stay focused. I might still be too weak to wiggle my toes or my fingers, but I know... *I just know*... that I can, at the very least, open my eyes. And if I can open my eyes... then I can finally see him...

And then, on one sunny Sunday, I do. At long last, I finally do open my eyes and once I do, I see a man with bright blonde hair staring back at me and smiling...

SNEAK PREVIEW #2:

My Life is a Soap Opera

CHAPTER 1

Election Night

"Just breathe, Katherine," my assistant, James Petruchio, tells me.

"It's not that bad," he attempts to console me, as he grabs a hold of my cold and sweaty palms.

"Really, it's not the end of the world," he says with a bright smile.

A smile that I wish could easily fade away and instead, be replaced with another form of darkness and bitterness that I currently feel brewing within my shattered heart.

"How can you continue to speak so positive about everything?" I ask him, while I simultaneously turn my head away from his gaze.

Currently, I'm sitting down on my green velvet chair, located inside of my home office, and trying my best not to have a nervous breakdown. As far as I'm concerned, my life might as well be over.

All of my dreams, ambitions and desires, it's all amounted to *nothing*. After spending the past ten years working in the world of politics, tonight, my career has finally come crashing down into the oblivion. My life as I've known it, is now officially *over…*

"So, you lost the election, big deal," James finally acknowledges the long-held truth, that I previously sought so hard to deny this past hour or so.

"It's not the end, but the beginning," he says with much passion and conviction. "You, Katherine Sharp, shall rise again."

"Really? And do what exactly?" I mock his optimistic kindness with the cruel pessimistic undertone of my voice.

"If I'm not the next Senator of California, then what was the point of it all?" I ask him, while also gazing directly into his hazel eyes. Eyes, that are as of right now, the only source of comfort that's holding my sanity together like glue.

"I might as well change my name and move to Alaska or better yet," I inform him, dramatically, "Relocate to a private island, floating out in the middle of the Aegean Sea. Because, if I'm not in politics anymore, then I'm no long Katherine Sharp!"

"Don't be foolish. Katherine, you are *not* married to the world of politics," he clicks his tongue, in disagreement. "The only reason that I'm still standing here in the shadows of politics, is because of *you*. If it wasn't for *your* strong will and determination, then I wouldn't have lasted all this time by your side."

And *that confession*, certainly, catches my attention. For the past three years, James has been my rock for everything. Without him, I'd simply be lost. He coordinates my meetings with donors, schedules my appointments with various doctors, sets aside time in my calendar to allow me to work out at the local gym and plus, he also plays the part of a dedicated chaperone to all of our public events as my sole partner in crime.

Overall, James knows my schedule *and* life better than I do.

Katherine Sharp might be the face and star of the show, but James Petruchio is the brains and heart behind the operations.

Additionally, after going through a host of personal assistants—many of whom, I fail to remember their names or faces in the first place— James is the only person, who can successfully withstand my strong and diva-like personality. As an upcoming female politician, many insiders in the press have nicknamed me as the *Shrew*, with James, being the only one who can tame me.

But as offensive as that term might seem to outsiders, it actually doesn't bother me in the least. I'd happily be the *Shrew*, if that's what it takes to rise up to power. Bowing down to no man, as I fight my ticket to the top.

However, tonight, I officially lost the election and now, everything that I worked so hard for, really was all for nothing. Perhaps, even this powerful shrew wasn't strong and charming enough to win over the hearts of the voters.

"Don't worry, Katherine," James says, as he kneels down in front of me.

Looking at him, I can't help but express a weary smile. James Petruchio might be my assistant, but he's also lovely in appearance, too.

With rich and wavy auburn and copper-like hair, hazel eyes with a thick set of lashes, a soft and fair complexion and a tall and muscular figure, he's a stark contrast to my petite self with medium length and straight black hair, porcelain fair skin and violet eyes. Plus, not to mention, the age difference between us. He might be seven years younger than I, but he acts so much older.

Regardless, one day, I hope that he can find someone who's worthy of him. After putting up with my selfish antics over the years, he certainly deserves a good woman who can truly appreciate him. He might be my angel, but I'm fairly certain that I'm his devil.

"But, James, it's all over," I whisper softly, biting the lower edge of my lip, as tears stream down my flushed cheeks. "I lost the election so badly. No donor will ever reinvest in me again. My career is finished."

"Trust me, Katherine, politics is not everything," James confides in me, wiping my tears away with his handkerchief. "After all, my father was a politician, too. Remember? This job requires thick skin, which we both already know that you've got and then some. But at the same time, this world is also just based on sex, lies and politics. Don't get too lost in this superficial bubble. You're capable of so much more."

That's true, James' father was a former politician. In fact, back in the day, I even interned for him. Out of all my close associates, James grew up in the world of political intrigue. It's one of the primary reasons as to why I originally hired him in the first place. But now, that past history, has all come crashing down into nothing.

"You know," I begin to reflect aloud, "I spent most of my youth dreaming of this night. From studying political science religiously at my university's library into the late midnight hours to associating with the right crowds, and even my own appearance, has been meticulously tailored to portray the perfect image of a proper female politician. Dark pants suits, with no color. And I *love* color! Especially, pastels!"

"I know you do," he sighs, as he runs his hand through his thick auburn hair. "Tomorrow, I promise that we'll go shopping and buy you a whole new wardrobe with a collection dedicated solely to pastel clothing. Afterwards, you can burn your other attires. In fact, we'll even throw a bon fire in your honor."

Shockingly, for the first time tonight since the election results originally came in, I finally laugh. As it turns out, I'm delighted by the prospect of burning the clothes that represents my now soon-to-be past. Clothes that I once foolishly associated as articles of my identity.

"You can always try again, too," he points out, remaining my ever the optimistic sidekick.

"No, there's no point," I acknowledge this sad and bitter truth. "James, I lost badly. By a landslide. Only wining thirty-seven percent of the overall votes. At this point, the statistics can't justify the means of me running again. Plus, if I'm being honest, I feel burnt out, too. I'm thirty-five years old now. I think I'd like to do something else. But then again, who I am, if I'm not involved in politics?"

It's true, the name Katherine Sharp has become synonymous as being an elite member of the political world. The public, the press, my peers, and even, my opponents, will always recognize me as the *Shrew*. Plus, I've spent the past ten years working in this cutthroat industry.

From graduate school to interning at the capital, to running a successful nonprofit and eventually, gaining the senate nomination. But regardless of all of these accomplishments; in the end, I still lost, no matter how promising my political career had seemed. Heck, even the polls had previously projected my win, only but a mere week ago. How foolish I was to think otherwise!

"Come, let's get you to bed," he finally changes the subject. "You've got an early appointment scheduled for tomorrow morning."

"But what about the broken glass?" I ask him, shamefully.

Unfortunately, hearing the news of my loss, sent me into a daze. One way or another, the crystal glass of champagne that I was previously holding, managed to find itself thrown across the room, slamming against the wall and shattering into pieces. Like my career, this broken glass can never, ever be recovered. From celebration to devastation.

"Katherine, you can't cry over spilled milk. It's time to let it go," he reminds me. "I'll order you a new set this week."

With that faithful promise, I finally head off to bed. Letting go of all my troubles and stress. At least, temporarily, for now.

ABOUT THE AUTHOR

Kristina Stangl is an American author. She was born and raised in San Francisco, California, USA. She holds a Master's degree in Public Administration, MPA; a Bachelor of Arts in International Relations, with a minor in Middle East and Islamic Studies from San Francisco State University; along with Teaching English as a Foreign Language (TEFL) credentials from the University of Toronto, Ontario Institute for Studies in Education. Before writing her first novel, Kristina previously worked in both the public and private sectors, having served in the United States federal government for nine years. In addition to writing, Kristina enjoys traveling across the globe and visiting famous and historical sites, which she documents on her social media accounts. To date, she has traveled to over thirteen countries, three continents, and speaks three languages. When Kristina is not traveling or writing, she's at home experimenting with baking new desserts, pies and other sweet treats.

www.ingramcontent.com/pod-product-compliance
Lightning Source LLC
Chambersburg PA
CBHW071432300726
48976CB00004B/1310